POL
INCORRECT
CHILDREN'S STORIES

Rough Stories for Tough Times

S. Ram Kumar

notionpress
.com

INDIA · SINGAPORE · MALAYSIA

Notion Press

Old No. 38, New No. 6
McNichols Road, Chetpet
Chennai - 600 031

First Published by Notion Press 2019

ISBN 978-1-64760-783-8

Dedication

Those to whom my deepest gratitude and thanks are due already know, in every which way.

Some do not and I salute them here:

- **Jackson Pollock** for showing what it takes to chart a completely new path, succeed beyond imagination, abandon it, and start another.
- **Russell Peters** and **Bill Burr** for showing how envelopes are malleable.
- **Kurt Godel** for the reassurance that Complete Consistency is a Chimera.
- **Col. Jim Corbett** for proving that you can be a Hunter, an Angler and a Naturalist at the very same time. And for all the stories, when I had none.
- **Taradiddlesmithy.com** may you flourish!!!

Contents

Acknowledgments

To my wife Dr Anupama for giving me the material (!) to write this book with and for all the rope in the world and beyond!!!

Acknowledgments

[illegible] ...wing was the [illegible] this book [illegible] ...ech
[illegible]

Preface/Introduction/Prologue

(Actually 'Read me first')
A Note on Politically Incorrect Children's Stories

- I have two children and when small, they needed bedtime stories. And the goons, they wanted original stories. In a fit of stupidity, I decided I would dream up the stories myself. Little did I realise what I was letting myself in for.
- These are stories made on the fly, in the sublime-anxious state of mind that can only be generated by:
    - A small child on each side
    - Inside a warm quilt
    - Winter or air conditioner delivered - super cold
    - Hard expectations of a corking good tale coming up.

  - The promise of my sleep based on success of the story!

- There are many tales that fell by the way. Critiques included poor structure, laziness in setting up the plot, too cootchie-pootchie, not funny enough. This critiquing business was taken up with so much zeal that there are times when one spent the whole day dreading story time!!!!
- On the flip side, the successful stories were so well received that the audience didn't go to sleep but demanded another. One was torn between the glow of critical acclaim and the pain of generating a new story.
- **These are not FMCG[1] tales that tax no faculty. These demand serious listening, contain unfamiliar words, concepts and contexts and constitute learning constructs outside just the tale. They are templates for learning. Hell, I learnt so much.**
- They are real, contemporary and hard. No sissy poo stuff, no pussyfooting. Children are extremely sophisticated customers, they can be.
- By the way, it is curious to see how customers are patronised:

---

[1] FMCG are Fast Moving Consumer Goods. Super easy and quick to bite, chew and reach for the next pack, say potato chips. Sugarcane is NOT FMCG!

  - If it is for Women, pink it and Shrink it [2]
  - If it is for Children- color it with the most garish colors, make the language infantile and, oh, load it with cartoon characters[3]

- There is a regular cast of characters and 'scapes' who are summoned at various times to lend depth and flavor

  - Bila sometimes Bilan
    - a Boy
  - Kabun
    - a Girl
  - Kolaa Raoo
    - Management expert
  - Mr Morkley
    - A dog that walked into Kabun's house and then called it home! It is not clear whether Kabun adopted Mr Morkley or vice versa.
  - PICS Dad
    - The Politically Incorrect Children's Story-monger

---

[2] https://www.washingtonpost.com/lifestyle/style/the-end-of-shrink-it-or-pink-it-a-history-of-advertisers-missing-the-mark-with-women/2016/06/08/3bcb1832-28e9-11e6-ae4a-3cdd5fe74204_story.html

Here's an example: Dell's cute Laptop: 'Della', which has nifty software for searching for recipes!!!

[3] See https://www.uxmatters.com/mt/archives/2011/10/effective-use-of-color-and-graphics-in-applications-for-children-part-i-toddlers-and-preschoolers.php as an example

- Ancientben – Hoarypast-Sethji Malikji School. A hypothetical school with a name similar to the archetype
    - Named after an ancestor known only to the school patriarch
    - From ancient history
    - A business group now venturing into the school business with 'giving back' to society as the mission!!!
- Manmath Kundu, a friend of mine from ancient times. He introduced me to the concept of pronunciation as a key to understanding language and dialects.

✦ These stories were really told to Bila and Kabun... Promise, ask them. They have now grown up and are making up their own stories. They do not need these any more. Thanks for wanting them.

The Epic, Intergalactic, Totally Universally Acceptable Story

"________________"

By
Bila and Kabun

Bila and Kabun were to write a story for their creative writing class.

Look up for the story. You don't believe it? Completely blank no? For there is another story behind that blank story. I'll tell you.

Originally it was a long and wonderful story. Full of adventure and surprise and mystery and intrigue and crime and mayhem and bad people and the ungodly and such adrenaline-pumping stuff..........

And this is what it was:

Jungle Mein Gadbad[4]

Once upon a time which is when all stories start, time stood still. Deep in the forest, there was a little log hut in which lived a woodcutter and his family. They had three children and a wild assortment of animals. There was a panther rescued as a cub. A little bear abandoned by its mother slept under the girl's bed. There was a donkey that the woodcutter used to move wood to and fro from the forest to the nearby city to sell. And there were a dozen more animals which would visit the woodcutter's house for food and to play with the children and to generally hangout. A badger, a python, a beaver, all kinds of birds and a particularly bad-tempered peacock who hated all other animals. The children had a great time playing with all these animals. The panther had grown big and all the other animals were afraid of him. Actually, he wanted to play but then if a hulking big panther jumps on you, who could imagine he wanted to play?!!!!!

The children named the Panther "*Sher Singh*[5]" Which was a wonderful, powerful name for such a magnificent animal. But they never could decide on names for the other animals. So the named them whatever they liked. This confused the animals crazily. So the girl called the bear *Ghatotkacha*[6], and the boys called him Saleeeeeeem and sometimes, Zareer. Now you would ask why so many 'e e e e e's' in Saleeeeeeem. That was because of how film stars

---

[4] Meaning trouble in the Jungle.

[5] *Sher* means Lion. *Singh* too means lion; a popular surname Therefore *Sher Singh* is one hell of a name.

[6] *Ghatotkacha*, from the Epic *Mahabharata,* a formidable warrior. Literally means Bald Pot.

spelled their names[7]. The Zareer was because it rhymed with career and the boy hoped that the bear would have a great career in the circus when it grew up. And because the python ate so much the boys called it "*Ghatotkacha*". Now you see the confusion. Calling *Ghatotkacha* could get you either the bear or the python!!!!

The bear slept under the girl's bed and when the nights got too cold it would slip into the girl's blanket!!!!!!! How warm and wonderful it was. So on cold nights, the girl would call "*Ghatotkacha*" and soon there would be one furry and one scaly creature fighting inside the blanket. And maybe a couple of squirrels and a monkey trying to slime their way into a warm, cozy situation.

Their parents would give them one *Anna*[8] each as pocket money every week. The girl bought a nice pink ribbon. She tied it on the panther and oh so smart he looked. The boys were annoyed and thought it was silly. So they went and bought a can of fluorescent red paint and painted the bear's tail red. This led to such a big fight that the forest started shaking. Just then the woodcutter came back after a long day's work and was entering the house. He was so tired that he had taken off his turban[9] and put it on his donkey's head. So the donkey was not able to see clearly and was weaving this way and that. The kids found it so funny that they

---

[7] A popular meme in which 'experts' advise changing the spelling of a name to achieve more traction.

[8] Anna, an old unit of currency, equal to 1/16 of an Indian Rupee or 6.25 paise. Anna Hazare is also the name of an ex-military person who is a very respected social and environmental activist.

[9] Turban – Traditional Headgear

started laughing and forgot all about their fighting....... and they stopped writing here.......... just here....

And so what a lovely funny story that was, but alas it was not to be.

1. The **Story Writers Association** complained that children are not allowed to write stories and that this story should be completely withdrawn.
2. The **Forests and Natural Resources Ministry** felt that the story insulted their work and made it look as if any woodcutter could cut wood in the best of National Parks. Besides all animals were protected under Wildlife Acts and no such pets as in the story were allowed and if it happened all would be prosecuted. Besides the title questioned their ability to manage the country's wild heritage. Was it not rude?
3. The **Political Parties** protested that the peacock was the National Bird[10] and writing about a bad-tempered one was anti-national. The whole country's image would be tarnished forever. A hartal[11] was planned for the next day.
4. The **Word-Moral Police** launched a campaign and said that the word "DONKEY" was inappropriate; even to describe donkeys. The correct word was "very slightly mentally challenged, extreme heavyweight carrying, underfed, kicking mammal with a loud horn".

---

[10] The Peacock is the National Bird of India

[11] *Hartal* – a form of protest

5. The **Physicians Association** protested that this bears sleeping in girl's beds was unhygienic and could lead to innumerable diseases that they were not even aware of. Such stories set a bad example to all children.
6. The **Urban Development Commission** wanted the story banned because they said the story posited that all cities existed basically to take wood from the forests and damage the environment. This hurt their image.
7. The **Nit-Pickers Guild** pointed out that the story could not exist at all because it was factually incorrect. How can you have a beaver, a panther and a python in the same story? Beavers live in North America and Panthers live in more equatorial countries. Besides "*Sher*" is for Lion and not panthers.
8. The **LGBT community** protested that this pink ribbon business portrayed all of them as animals.
9. The **Sports Association** condemned the story and said the playing was only for sports people. Panthers playing with people and other animals denigrated their very image.
10. **All Religious Communities** roundly condemned the story and complained that the names given to the animals were not acceptable and insulted their religious leaders, places of worship, icons, symbols, sacred books, and beliefs. They also said the story hurt much more than their sentiments:

what exactly they were not immediately sure of, but it hurt like hell.

11. An **Anti-Cruelty Coalition** protested that the bears cannot be sent to circuses. This story was dragging us back to the middle ages.
12. The **Astrology-Numerology-Vaastu-FengShui-Tantra** and other assorted non-scientific pursuits organization flatly objected to using extra 'eees'. Only their association members were allowed to make such precise changes.
13. The **Printers Union** decried the authors for using so many 'e's. Such irresponsible use of alphabets would mean that the whole country's resources of alphabets would be depleted. More would have to be imported depleting the country's foreign exchange reserves and lead to a severe economic recession.
14. The **Environmentalists** were up in arms. They had not read the story but knew vaguely that some wood, animals, and children were involved. So they decided to do a preventive march – just in case.
15. Meanwhile, the **Exotic Animals Association** was pissed off that they had not been asked to approve a draft and wanted to know why rhino, hippopotami[12] and elephants were not included.
16. The **NGOs** were in a tizzy. Why were the children not going to school? That was against the Right To Education – a signature campaign was launched.

---

[12] Yes, YES, technically the plural of Hippopotamus IS Hippopotami!!! Of course, you can also say Hippos.

17. The **Mythological Film Producers Association** complained that using mythical character names out of context was rude and hurt them at various places.
18. The **Anna Hazare Team**[13] was annoyed: this pocket money business was an affront to their work. There was only one ANNA and parents offering each of their children one ANNA each week was ridiculous.
19. The **Timepiece and Clock Manufacturers Association** wanted to take Bila and Kabun to court for defaming the quality of timekeeping devices, indeed defaming time itself by saying it stood still. They suggested that the story be amended to include the following lines: "time went tick-tock perfectly and all clocks, watches, timepieces, alarm clocks, grandfather clocks, clocks in homes, hospitals, railway stations, airports, stadia, public places, etc. were working perfectly".
20. The **Graffiti – Street Art alliance** was up in arms and saw the story as a grave insult to their style of vandalism …er profession. Spray painting bears' tails showed them in a very bad artistic light.
21. **All Minority and Majority religious leaders** protested that a turban is a strong, revered symbol and no one should place it on a Donkey no matter how tired they are.

---

[13] Ibid. (means quoted before in another footnote)

22. Immediately the **Moral Word Police** launched an agitation against the Religious leaders for using the word "donkey". Did they not know the correct word: "very slightly mentally challenged, extreme heavyweight carrying, underfed kicking mammal with a loud horn"?

So Bila and Kabun were flabbergasted by over twenty or so agitations, *hartals, fast-to-death pandals, relay hunger strikes, morchas, gheraos, bandhs, signature campaigns, marches, and candlelight vigils*[14] outside their studio. Sighing wearily, they edited, cut, changed, compressed and sanitized their story to suit all the groups. Here it is:

"______________"

By Bila and Kabun

···— –··· – – ··– –·– ·– — ·–· —–··· – – ··– –·– ·– — ·–·— –··· – –
··– –·– ·– — ·–···· – – ··– –·– ·– — ·–· — –··· – – ··– –·– ·– — ·–·—
–··· – – ··– –·– ·– — ·–···· – – ··– –·– ·– — ·–· — –··· – – ··– –·– ·–
–·– ·– — ·–·— –··· – – ··– –·– ·– — ·–···· – – ··– –·– ·– — ·–· — –···
–·– ·– — ·–· — –··· –·– ··– –·– ·– — ·–·— –··· – – ··– –·– ·– — ·–·

[14] All forms of protests with varying degrees of locomotion, violence, impact and silliness. For instance, a relay hunger fast involves people taking turns to not eat!!!!! That's what ALL of us do every single day!!!

PS: Shortly after publishing this version, Bila and Kabun were stunned to find the **Morse Code Association** picketing outside their studio against improper use of their symbols.

Now you know why the story is BLANK!!!

A Really Short Story

PICS dad woke up Bila and Kabun. It was time to go home. He had already packed up his stuff.

The kids were still at it. iPod, iPad, Solar Charger, Torches, headlamps, mosquito repellent, can opener, assorted foodstuff, drawing stuff, camera equipment, books, backpacks, towels, bath stuff, toothpaste and brush, shoes, socks, underwear, belt, windcheater, sleeping bags, sunglasses, telescope, binoculars, matches, compass, paints, sketch pens and pencils, portable stove, fuel for stove and lantern, lantern, hunting knife, Swiss knife, cell phones, inflatable pillows, water bottles, glo-sticks[15], first aid kit, specimen bottles, field guides for mammals, insects, birds, and fish, cooking pan, kettle, coffee mugs, rope……

PICS dad yelled again for them to move their butts, and an hour later Bila and Kabun were ready to go. Loaded up

[15] Glo-Stik, Snap them and they glow

the massive 4 X 4 pickup truck, and before they drove off, Bila and Kabun wondered if they had left anything behind: maybe the USB or the external hard drive, wallets, kerchiefs, bandannas, sweatbands, screwdriver?

Oh…fish…hope nothing left behind. Hope they had put out the fire. Hope their keys were with them…. despite all a ten-day camp was fun indeed.

And they whistled for Mr. Morkley. Mr. Morkley came up running up to the 4X4 and leaped in, tail wagging furiously. He did have a few extra ticks but was ready to roll. Even his collar was not really his, Kabun had put it on.

END OF STORY!!!!

Animal School

Bila and Kabun were camping in the forest. After a hard day's trekking, they were cooking food and delicious aromas were wafting around the jungle. The warm fire also looked so cozy in the cold, in fact, freezing night.

Bila and Kabun jumped when a small furry creature climbed up Bila's and then Kabun's shoulder. It was a squirrel. He ate a few bread crumbs and then fell asleep near the fire. They moved him away from the fire onto a big tarp[16] to make sure he would not get singed. Minutes later there was an otter and then a pair of gibbons, all toasting in the warmth of the fire. They refused bread and biscuits and peanuts. Bila and Kabun realized the animals had not come for the food, they had come for the warmth. But their behavior and pregnant silence also told them there was another reason.

[16] (Tarpaulin)

Bila and Kabun had a strange feeling. You see both of them had not been 'exercising' for quite some time and had become, well, a little "large – economy "sized. Hmmm, were the animals ganging up to, well…? Is this why they were refusing peanuts and biscuits and wanted to eat something else???!!!!!

By the time Bila and Kabun finished their dinner and were having their customary Ecuadorian Coffee, they were surrounded. Panthers, elephants, tigers, anteaters, badgers, sambar, chital, cobras, sand boas, monitor lizards, peacocks, jungle fowl, fishing eagles and great horned owls were gathered ALL around them. And all were silent and peacefully resting one way or another, except the elephants which remained standing as they always do.

And so Bila and Kabun activated their DIGINIMALs (see the DIGINIMAL Story for details) and then said to the animals "we hope you come in peace". And then they got so embarrassed and quite glowed red with shame… Because the great horned owl and the Jungle hare both came to the clearing on the back of the old *Dhole*[17] and said "Bila and Kabun, our true friends, we come here in peace, not to eat each other but to seek your advice. You both never hurt ANY of us and Kabun is so kind to so many of us."

"We came to ask you how come Humans are so smart? We Jungle folk would also like to become smart. We think people folk are so smart because they have schools". Their redness didn't show because it was so dark, but Bila and Kabun put more wood on the fire to make it warmer,

[17] *Dhole* = Indian Wild Dog, Dingo = Australian Wild Dog, African Wild Dog = Painted Lycaon

especially for the elephants which were so far away. And then they said, "How can we help you"?

And so the animals said they had made a committee and realized that the reason people were so smart was that they went to school... so could you help us set up a school too? A Jungle School!!!

And Bila Kabun said yes!!!!!!!!!!!!!!!!!!!!!!

They explained that "school" or "teaching-learning" so looonggg ago was in the hands of religion. Madrasas had learned men teaching reading and writing through the Holy Quran to Moslem children; The Christian Church taught divinity and religious learning to acolytes and Hindu Gurukuls taught language, religion, and rituals to *shishyas*[18]. This was a highly regulated and stratified process that only a few could access.

About 500 years ago, learning shifted to Monarchy: where Royal courts around the world, be it Moslem, Hindu, Christian, or whatever saw to it that teaching-learning occurred-but to a very select community/ communities.

Some 150 years ago it shifted to "governments" and they decided degrees, conferment, certifications and whatever. But then again it was a funnel through which few could pass and was not available to everyone. School, the most basic, was meant to provide cannon fodder for the industrial revolution; everybody needs to come on time, wear the same dress, and do the same thing, the school teaches you this, so you can then go work in a

[18] Students

factory..... This is what millions have been conditioned on for decades....

Now, NOW it has shifted to private hands and whoever can pay can learn. Never mind whether they can learn or not. If you can pay you get 'certified'.

After this BIG philosophical lecture, all the animals nodded including the squirrels who were fast asleep and together chorused "we want a school". So then Bila and Kabun asked "Why us? Do it yourself. "Then the poor animals said, "we tried, we know you would have asked us this, so we tried". But when the panther and the badger went to the school near the National Park, all the teachers, students, attendants, security guards, forest rangers with BIG mucchis[19] and big guns ran away, scared to death. "We could barely ask a single question... So will you please help us...???!!!"

So Bila and Kabun said yes.... So over the next three months, they helped the animals. And this was what happened. Remember the "Animal School Committee" consisted of the badger, panther, *Dhole*, Jungle hare, great horned owl at the very least. And poor Bila and Kabun had to smuggle them into schools around the country in backpacks and burlap sacks to get them to 'research' first-hand how a school works!!!!!!!!!!!!!

So here's what they found:

- School Libraries first need cupboards with huge locks – never mind that libraries are designed to

[19] *(Mucchi* = Moustache)

help students take books. The main purpose is security. If the keys can be lost – even better

- Uniforms need to be of crappy material, that way students would need to buy more of them. And the Uniform supplier will be some crony of the Ancientben-Hoarypast-Sethji-Malikji family ecosystem.
- All sports supplies will be locked. This is so that no one can 'spoil' them.
- Classes will be held for 40 minutes each. So the moment someone develops an interest in a subject, they can be pulled off and shifted to something else.
- Swimming pools will be filled for the publicity brochure. After that, they can be drained for safety reasons.
- Teachers will be recruited at really poor pay. This ensures that only the most desperate end up as teachers. Those who are truly motivated will fade away over the years.
- School food will be of the lowest grade imaginable. It will be unhygienic, inedible and unhealthy. To keep kids happy it will have absolutely "non-food-item- numbers" like bhajiyas[20] and pakodas[21].
- School busing is a place to make money. So the school bus will have signs like "this is a precious school bus carrying invaluable citizens of the

---

[20] (Fritters, somewhat like Tempura)

[21] More Fritters, (somewhat like more Tempura).

future, if it is driving erratically, please call &&*&(&*)(%@$@#%@, which invariably is an invalid number because the poor, hapless transport manager's prepaid number has run out of balance. And the buses are claptrap and driven by those who cannot become well paid private taxi drivers.

- Camps can be organized to inveigle unsuspecting parents to send children to unnecessary and irrelevant activities. Besides parents just want to get pesky children out of the way and ANYTHING is OK.
- Absolutely inane topics and issues like the independence movement and martyrs will be taken to stage MEGA plays. Nobody believes in them, the parents bust their balls to make the costumes, classes are lost, and the children have absolutely no interest but it makes the school look good in brochures.
- School children have to be sent to absolutely worthless events like the "Bhutadijhapa International Golf Tournament" in which only TWO and a HALF schools participate in so that ALL are guaranteed a medal. Ditto for electrocution[22], Fizz[23], Probate[24] and so on.

---

[22] Pun Intended

[23] Pun Again intended

[24] And yet again

- Make book fairs META events along with school day or PTA[25] day or whatever so that extremely crappy books can be sold with a hefty school commission which naturally goes into the Ancientben-Hoarypast-Sethji-Malikji family trust.
- Make children do completely 'un-sustained' (not unsustainable) activities like a vegetable garden, tree plantation, etc. purely as a photo-op.
- Talk about stuff that is TOTALLY not practiced. Like in the class talk about hygiene and sanitation while the school toilets are utterly dirty. Talk about nutrition and balanced diets while serving crap in the mess. And of course, the school drinking water is unfit to drink.
- Do outreach stuff that is TOTALLY unrelated to on-ground reality: Newsletters, School Networks for Excellence; Teacher Awards; Bravery Awards; Best Entrepreneur Awards; NGOs for underprivileged children.... for biodata and brochure value ALONE.
- Make uniforms complex with belts, blazers, stockings, fleur-de-lis, cravats, bow ties, scabbards, cod-pieces, lances, shields, escutcheons, body-armor, garters, ties, socks, langots[26] and so on so that the family lackey at the supplies shop of the Ancientben-Hoarypast-Sethji-Malikji family makes tons of money.

---

[25] Parent Teacher Association

[26] (Traditional Athletic Supporter)

- Extra smart schools also include stuff like scouts and guides, NCC, French Legion, American SEALS, Russian KGB, Gestapo, NKVD, SAS, Mossad, and other such exotic stuff purely to sell more uniforms and gear.
- All schoolbooks, notebooks, bags, pencils, pencil-leads, pens, ink, geometry boxes, covers, labels, bag-lint, etc will ALL have to be bought at the front man's in-school shop of the Ancientben-Hoarypast-Sethji-Malikji family.
- Charge peanuts for the tuition fee and make money on transport, food, uniforms, supplies, camps, outreach, activities and any such stuff you can dream of. So Tax-free and rest is MOOLAH in the pocket.
- Of course, school finishes at three. But parents do not get home till 6.00 so devise absolutely unnecessary and obsolete activities like German and French Language, Crochet, Bead Counting, Sand Sifting, Basket Weaving, SUPW (don't ask me) and so on to kill time and charge for it. Smart schools put in stuff like the theory of r/c plane flying, theoretical nuclear reactor design, drawings of mountain climbing, understanding space travel which while conveying extreme adventure are basically pure whitewash.
- Classrooms should have CCTV, riot control guns, teargas dispensing systems, and other stuff. But it should be badly lit, have poor furniture, creaky

boards, sad teachers, bad/non-existent ventilation and a horrible smell.

And when the Animal Committee saw all this and saw the REAL story with Bila and Kabun they decided that they were better off without an Animal School at all. They were so disillusioned.

But Schools apart, could they come and cuddle up by the fire whenever Bila and Kabun were around?

That's why even today you will find no (real) animals in school but tons of them willing to cuddle up by you near the fire……

Best of Breed, Friend in need and all that sort of thing….

Girlie Cata[27] had a BIG problem. BIG BIG Problem. Actually small, tiny problem. But a BIG problem … no small problem…oh, fish. The problem was BIG; the reasons were small…. The small reasons were two tiny little kittens. The BIG problem was that the roof had caved in!!!!! The floor too. Everything!!! And now it was all wet, muddy, cold and annoying.

You see instead of 'doing' kittens under the warm bed or in the loft in Kabun's house, Girlie Cata had 'done' the kittens in the society's huge common garden. Just under the stone sitting bench. Why? Silly goose, actually silly cat she was. At her 'kitty' party all the other hi-society cats had warned her against Mr. Morkley. He was, to use the phrase

[27] (Cata = Cat)

of an NGO that cared for dogs, was not a "private[28]" dog. He was a 'street' dog. A mongrel, a mutt, like Obama once described himself. "Private dogs "were all those fancy shmancy Poodles and Dachshunds, Terriers and Labradors and Alsatians, great Danes and so on. You know, all those smart dogs with fancy collars, shampooed hair and their noses in the air. Mr. Morkley was just a poor dog that walked into Kabun's house one day. And Mr. Morkley liked nothing better than a nice dip in some muddy dirt, a couple of quick mock fights with his street friends, some wild running around like crazy, a little barking practice at the milkman or newspaperman and of course sniffing every car tire in sight – for their exotic smells carried from far, far away… Of course chasing cats was fun too. And so Girlie Cata wanted nothing to do with this trashy Mr. Morkley.

And so the silly Girlie Cata did not want to "do" kittens in Kabun's house, she wanted to do it in an "exclusive place". So she chose the bench near which all the society big-time hoity-toity women did their YOGA (read: gossiping while relaxing in Shavasan[29]) in the mornings. According to what this silly cat had heard these even sillier women say – everything had to be "earthy, natural, environment-friendly and green". Getting all mixed up, Girlie Cata, in a little burrow under the stone bench, bought two sweet little kittens into this bad, mad, world.

---

[28] Private Dog = Dogs with pedigree e.g.: Labrador, Alsatian, Pug, Irish Setter

[29] This is the easiest of Yoga poses, just lie down and super relax. Difficult to discern from regular sleeping!

And then it rained so hard the ground gave way, the burrow caved in, really deep, and the place was all wet, muddy, cold and messy. So Girlie ran to her "kitty party" friends for help. All of them said it was too wet, and muddy and it would make their tails droop and spoil their nail polish and whiskers and of course they would be glad to help NEXT summer!!!!!

Poor Girlie ran to all the hifalutin' dogs for help. Imagine a cat asking purebred, show-dogs for help. "Get lost," they all said to the last man, well, dog, "we the bourgeoisie do not truck with the proletariat". Girlie Cata understood none of this except for the "do not" part.

Desperately she looked around for Kabun, but she was away at school. So what to do? Just as she was leaving Kabun's house, Mr. Morkley spied her tail around the corner and gave chase. When he rounded the corner, he was stunned to see Girlie walking slowly. Annoyed at having his chase fizzle out, Mr. Morkley barked loudly putting extra emphasis on the hi-tone at the end, which meant 'cats beware, canine cat hunting caliph – Mr. Morkley is on the prowl". At this Girlie sat down. Mr. Morkley shook his head and went back round the bend, wanting to start the action all over again. He emerged from the bend barking wildly to find Girlie still sitting on the ground. Puzzled, he sat down next to her, a safe distance away from her sharp teeth and claws.

He asked in a low growl, "what's up?" And in a sad mewling voice she told him. Mr. Morkley was happy to help. He was absolutely delighted when he saw the caved in muddy burrow and saw what an excellently mud-splashy time could be had. Plus, there was no way Kabun could scold him – he got muddy saving lives no???!!!

In Mr. Morkley dived into the mud and was wallowing around till Girlie reminded him that perhaps there was some work to be done. On hearing this, Mr. Morkley perked up his ears and began listening intently for mews. Aha there they were and Mr. Morkley dived in ….and ……. disappeared.

Girlie was alarmed till Mr. Morkley came out after a few minutes with two muddy fur balls. He wouldn't part with them and ran back to his house. Kabun, who had just come back from school, was speechless when she saw what appeared to be a large ball of mud walking across to her making mewing AND growling noises. When she saw this was not part of a muddy ditch come alive but Mr. Morkley with two tiny kittens in his mouth, she was very angry with him. But then when Girlie started purring and rubbing herself against Mr. Morkley, things became a little clear. Some good deeds had happened and therefore the purring she guessed.

She left it to Girlie to clean up her babies and get to some warm place because Mr. Morkley was dragging her back into the rain and the bench. What she saw, flabbergasted her. A tunnel had opened up under the bench. She ran back to fetch Bila and some equipment: ropes, a fishing spool with tough monofilament, headlamps and a shovel. Then they followed Mr. Morkley who started with a mud bath as a sort of 'inauguration of the adventure'. Then they all crawled into the tight little hole which soon opened up into a slightly bigger tunnel. They tied the fishing line to a jutting rock to use as a guide to get back and kept going. A little later they could walk upright and the air was much colder and danker. They couldn't go further since they had run out of filament. So the muddy trio made their way back topside. Mr. Morkley was sternly warned against any more mud baths.

When the neighbors saw the muddy group there was much whispering and "ghusur-phusur"[30]. They were convinced that the kids had found some treasure. Immediately the Society office bearers and members swung into action and demanded that the treasure be handed over to the society for 'safekeeping'. Patiently PICS dad explained to the morons, er, members gathered that

A. No treasure had been found

B. Even if was; gold, silver, diamond, copper, tin, bismuth, petroleum.... whatever, it legally belonged to the Government by law. You only owned the land you built your houses on; the air above and what lay below always belonged to the Government.[31]

But the Members were adamant. They wanted to see and confirm. So the party set off: Mr. Morkley very much in the mood to continue his muddddddy frenzy. With great reluctance, the society honchos looked at the mud hole and wondered if there was a four-lane expressway through which they could drive inside without getting their clothes dirty or paying some "toll fees"!!! Sighing reluctantly two of them

---

[30] (whispered gossip).

[31] In India

followed the PICSgang into the "under-the-bench-land". So with plenty of safety line, the group made its way past the point where Bila and Kabun had turned back. The tunnel opened up and then it was big enough to walk in upright. And then it opened into a largish cavern. Full of stalactites and stalagmites, the cavern reflected light in myriad colors. A small stream flowed along its sides. It didn't take them long to explore it and then suddenly Mr. Morkley started chasing – a bat!!! Instantly Bila and Kabun knew that there must be an opening somewhere, otherwise, how could the bat have come in? A quick look around revealed a few insects and spiders and the stream was sure to contain some forms of life. Maybe later....

The Members of the society were getting bored. They did not see any secret room or treasure chest and this place was cold and smelt horrible and it had NO restaurants or coffee shops. So they wanted OUT....

After a couple of hours, all of them made their way back topside. Bila, Kabun and Mr. Morkley were bursting with excitement. PICS dad was just waiting to get the 'Spelunker's[32] guide to survival and identification of plants, birds, mammals, insects, spiders and fish' so he could help Bila and Kabun make a proper study/presentation. Suddenly all their excitement, enthusiasm and other overcharged emotions and energies were brought to a dazzling stop.

The two society members were speaking. "Nothing in there. Dirty, cold, smelly. No treasure chest, no indication of some old secret room or whatever. Total waste of time.

---

[32] Spelunking, to do with exploring the underground, especially caves.

We could have spent the time playing "Antakshari[33]". What a waste. No point in going in there".

And the PICSgang thought, right, 'no treasure in there – only stalactites, stalagmites, ancient limestone formations, maybe, just maybe, unknown species of plants, birds, mammals, insects, spiders and fish. And the chance to see where the cave system led back topside. And the excitement, and the rush of adrenaline and the chance to draw a cave map. A real NEW cave map. Absolutely no treasure. Only a dirty cold cave with nothing of value'.

The only thought in Mr. Morkley's head when he was being hosed down was "how do I get back to that wonderful mud again???!!!" No one noticed the tiny flecks of dazzling light reflected from some of the 'Mr. Morkley's' mud going down the drain......

---

[33] A game in which one sings a song and the other team has to sing a song starting with the last letter of the one just sung.

DIGINIMAL[34] – The Ultimate Pet

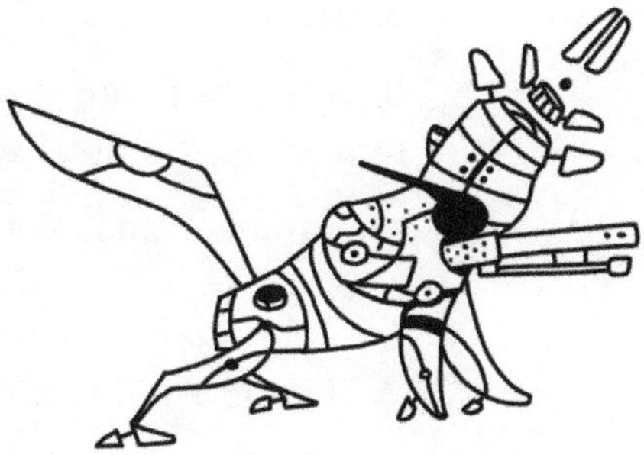

This is a dream pet story - a pet to play with and a pet to reckon with!!!! The idea is:

A. we all have pet[35] peeves.
B. They can be neutralized with an appropriate animal
C. Why not combine all 'peeves' with all possible solutions to create a super-duper 'DIGINIMAL'

It is an all-purpose project:

- As a science project
- Defence and offense project (Every country has a defence ministry. None has an offense ministry. So if every country is defending itself, then who the hell is carrying out the offense????!!!!!
- Pet project (chuckle chuckle)

[34] Digital + Animal = DIGINIMAL

[35] Pun intended

- To create a REAL PET. Not a sissy poo doggie, cat or parrot.
- It is a composite you see of mind, skill and technology – Animal and Human.
- A creature of land, wind, water, and mind….

  - It has claws, THE CLAWS. One set of claws like an echidna with poison and the other the awesome tearing claws of a bald eagle.
  - It has the ultra-strong beak (!) of the parrotfish!!!
  - It has the bone-cracking jaws of the hyena.
  - The thumb-splitting punch of the mantis shrimp
  - Zoom zoom speed of the tuna. Hey, the cheetah is fast but for a few seconds. The tuna can cruise for hundreds of kilometers at 60 kmph and can zip along at a hundred kmph!!!!
  - It has a prehensile tail like an elephant's trunk.
  - It has the heavy-duty muscles of an orangutan
  - The exceptional eyesight of a peregrine falcon.
  - The can smell 5 km up in the air like the nose of an Andean condor.
  - The industrial strength wings of an albatross.
  - The replaceable ever-growing razor-sharp teeth of a great white shark. And a pouch with the toxic saliva of the Komodo Dragon.

- Three horns: two wickedly curving Oryx horns and the third one from the narwhal: pointy and made of ivory.
- The color-changing abilities of a chameleon
- The massively toxic venom of the stonefish
- The fur of a sloth. Normally the sloth moves so slowly that algae and toxic bacteria grow in its fur. And stinks!!
- The hypersensitive ears of a bat along with a dolphin's echolocation.
- The sixth sense, the lateral line of fishes
- The unparalleled fearlessness and never-never-ever give up attitude of a honey badger

Now in addition to these, it has technology too:

- 1 dozen heat deflecting flares
- 16 mm twin machine guns
- 1 billion candle power external head-mounted searchlight – to search and stun
- External supersonic rocket pods
- Forward-Looking Infrared Radar
- Grenade pods in MetalStorm[36] format (firing at 500,000 rounds a second)
- SatNav communication and GPS systems for navigation, communication, and hunt/destroy missions.

---

[36] See www.metalstorm.com

- Solar and Mini-Nuclear power pack
- Microwave/RF jammer and 1 mini-neutron bomb to fry enemy communication.
- Sound Jammers
- 1 teraflop supercomputer
- Quantum Computer code making and breaking systems
- Erasable Programmable Profile Generation system. This will automatically create voice and face recognition, physical and infrared detection profiles to recognize specific enemy/avoidance targets. Then appropriate countermeasures with biological and/or other weaponry and systems will be carried out. Currently, these profiles are active for the following:

    - Painful Principals who give mind-numbingly boring speeches.
    - Kolaa Raoo
    - Painful Relatives, especially cousins
    - All Ponderous Borers[37]
    - They, who want "one bite" out of whatever you are eating.
    - People who lower the volume when you are listening to thumping music.
    - People who ask achingly moronic obvious questions like "are you having a bath?"

---

[37] Check the story "PICS Dad plays Judo

when you are in the bathroom or "are you jogging?" when you are covered in sweat doing 16 kmph.

- People who stand up and keep standing in the row in front when you are watching a movie.
- People who pretend to talk on cell phones.
- People who separate the pages from newspapers.
- He Who Must Not Be Named 1,2,3,4,5..n
- She Who Must Not Be Named 1,2,3,4,5..n
- And others....

When the DIGINIMAL is finally ready will let you know.......

Not Getting Mad, Getting Even

Bila and Kabun were foxed. They had heard about "RAGE". People driving, not always obeying the rules and then mayhem. The hormone-charged types honk, cut corners, stare at you and suggest impossible biological experiments with close relatives!!! The others do incredibly rash driving. Road rage, Air Rage, general rage – it is a Delhi thing, a Rome thing, a New York thing, a Cairo thing....it is an all-world thing. RAGE

Also lifts, cinema queues...everywhere. Lots of RAGE: road rage, film rage, elevator rage...... all types of rage.

So they asked PICSdad what to do.......and he advised them, do not get mad, get even!!!!!!!!! So here goes the story...

Be a shark at the park

See what happens at every parking lot:

You get in, into a crowded parking lot, and drive in for ages searching for a free spot. Eventually, you find one, park, everyone gets off, you switch off the engine, lock the car and then leave. Just then the parking lot attendant lands up and says "not here" and points to a different slot. For God knows what reason. Happens all the while. So what to do? PARKING RAGE??

No, get even. PICSdad says: Get everyone off, but just the driver (you) stays inside the car and DUCKS. Yes, ducks! When the parking lot guy appears, looking confused, jump up, look him in the eye and say "where do I park". The fact that you are not inconvenienced, searching for your keys, starting the car again and parking the car somewhere else is bound to unsettle the guy so much that you will get EVEN!!!!

The Ele-Waiter Trick

At every elevator, ***there*** is a queue. And when the elevator is just about full, the next guy wants to get in. And the elevator guy gets a BIG kick out of telling the next guy NOT to get in with a BIG MOUTZKA[38] gesture. Elevator RAGE???

No, get even. So when you are in the elevator line, wait and sense the situation. Even if your turn comes, wait!!!! Let the next guy get in. DO NOT ALLOW THE ELEVATOR GUY to use the Moutzka gesture even if it means missing two trips. Three of four trips will sort him out to distraction!!!!!!!!! Do not get mad, get even…

---

[38] Somewhat like a STOP sign, the MOUTZKA sign is very offensive in some cultures.

Give the secretary the BIRD!!!

Secretaries are technically called "Gatekeepers". And their job is to keep unwanted people OUT. So their basic idea is to intimidate, bully and make people feel they are unwanted!!! That is what very very busy BIG bosses want. So secretaries like to keep you waiting. And the big bosses, those big-time men, and women LOVE it because it makes them look bigger!!!!! So what do you do? Tantrum? Waiting RAGE???

NO. Get even. Greet the secretary very VERY pleasantly. Ask for the washroom, wash up and get fresh. Sink into the sofa with pleasure. Sprezzy[39] people have been known to take off their shoes and socks and put on soft slippers!!!. Pull out from your bag (you need to organize this) a BIG FAT BOOK, moisturizing lotion, and some snacks! Sit back, lean comfortably. Feel comfortable. Loosen tie, fold-back cuffs. Start reading. Make noises of pleasure like "Aaah and ooh". Polite secretaries might ask: "Can I get you some tea/ coffee?". Answer "Both". And SETTLE down.

NO SECRETARY CAN STAND A COMFORTABLE VISITOR for more than nanoseconds!!!!! He/she will see to it that you get in instantly!!!! Do not get mad, get even!!!!!!!!!!!!!!!

Road rage wet down!

And then for the road rage guy honking and blinking his lights behind you (not being sexist, it is always a man…). This one has a hit rate of, say, 10% but is worth it. The pleasure will make you smile for years. It also needs planning

---

[39] Sprezz The Art of Effortless Superiority from a book of the same name by Janey Preger.

and clockwork coordination. It works best on lonely country roads, single-lane, no space to overtake.

AT the word "go" from PICSdad,

A. Everyone slides down their windows
B. Puts their hands out and waves like mad for the guy to overtake.
C. Everyone's expressions must be abject, distilled horror. (E.g.: Poltergeist watching The Omen during Texas Chainsaw Massacre with The Blair witch Project in the background
D. Meanwhile, PICS dad organizes the Hazard lights, all light beams, a little brake lights, and some heavy brake squeal. He too will slide down his windows and wave the honker on with "folded" hands[40] as his car passes by!!!!!!

This drives the honky-road rage guy nuts. He is now convinced that a 6000-meter cliff or some such thing has opened right in front and that's why this terrified family is giving way. Drawn and guided by your collective horror, a premonition takes his mind over, he will forget to see the road ahead and not only brake frantically, with luck he will also wet his pants.

He would have stopped a hundred meters ahead. Now drive slowly past him with a collective quizzical look on your face – like you discovered that the Omen, Poltergeist, Texas gang and Blair witch folk are singing Christmas Carols. An enigmatic and beatific smile is also helpful – on ALL your faces.

---

[40] Gesture of greeting but in this case abject submission.

This accomplishes several things

a. He wet his pants
b. His road rage has been smothered
c. The extraordinary difference in your behavior would make him wonder whether he is going crazy.
d. Bonus: the next time he will honky-lights flash someone in road rage mood, Pavlov's[41] theory says he will wet his pants again.

Top the Cops

Traffic Cops stop you on the road and shake you down mentally, physically and sometimes economically. Considering that the Roads and Bullock Carts Transports and Shipchandling Act was written in the Jurassic Age, there are a million ways in which you could have transgressed it. For example

- Your bells to warn pedestrians are not working
- Your horse-whip is not in good condition
- You do not have a mandatory "dog-peeking-out-from-under-a-curtain" OR "Football-window-crash" sticker at the back.
- No yellow strip on roadside headlamps – why this is needed or works on a million candlepower xenon lights is a mystery.
- Singing while driving.
- The font on the license plate is not allowed.

[41] The dog and food thingy

So a determined bunch could catch you on one or the other thing even if you have your license, registration book, marriage certificate, blood test, are sober, are wearing a seat belt and a helmet, have a PUC[42] sticker, and a favorite religious figure stuck on top of your dashboard complete with pulsating, Technicolor lights. If it is the Official Collection Drive then they will "*challan*[43]" you. If it is festival time, then ....

You could do two things. One is a rip-off from an International ad. When the cops stop your car, usually two or three of them will herd you to make sure you do not drive off. Get your daughter at the back to flash a BIG card signed "help I am being kidnapped". The problem with this is that in addition to the normal "payment", you might be asked for a cut of the ransom. On the other hand, it can create quite a scene.

The other is more workable if you have the time and are keen on getting even, not mad. Stop the car politely. And make sure people are watching.

A. Ask the policeman for his ID. YES, HIS ID. This should freak him out. Tell him lots of con-men are now posing as Police, CBI[44], Income Tax[45] and whatnot. Where is his id? That should get him witless. If they persist and point to their Official Vehicle with a pot-bellied Inspector sitting inside, then.

---

[42] PUC = Pollution Under Control

[43] (Traffic Ticket)

[44] Central Bureau of Investigation, something like the FBI

[45] Like the IRS

B. You HAVE pre-planned. Pull out a military jacket with tons of medals, a military looking cap in red, gold and green and whisper confidentially in his ears that you are Emperor Haile Selassie, Rasta King. Let the Bob Marley play on loud and tell him you are licensed by god to smoke ganja. If he can come to Ethiopia, you can do dreadlocks for him – *kya bolta hai (Addis) a baba*[46]? Keep it going. Segue into plan …

C. Set your phone to video recording and put it on the roof. Say into the device. "senior reporter Outrik Bhattacharjee reporting from *Hafta Chowk*[47]. This is an encounter of a different kind". (the best, most argumentative press folk are always Bengali".) And let it roll…. if you have played it right, you will roll too, roll on buddy, and tell the police escort jeep where you want to go, lights, siren and all. They will only be too glad to guide you as far away as possible.

Never get mad. Get even.

Sweet Revenge

Who hasn't run out of change/coins? At vending and ticketing machines, faced with deserving pan-handlers & buskers, and donation boxes & envelopes we have run out. But we never paid with toffees, have we?

---

[46] This is in Hindi (In India, many people speak Hindi, not 'Indian'!!.) Transliterates to what you are reading.

[47] Translates to 'incentive' crossroads.

And so at the toll plaza and the restaurant and in the local grocery shop, they run out of coins and they pay us in toffees. Hang on, the math doesn't work out. If the friendly toll guy gives you a Rs[48] 1 toffee instead of Rs.1 then there is a problem. He gets the toffee for much less, say, 80 paise. So he is returning you 20% less. Next time you hit the toffee giving toll plaza, or restaurant or supermarket, choose peak time. Stop at the toll booth, checkout counter or whatever and hand him over a neat plastic zip-lock bag labelled "28 Toffees= Rs 28" or whatever the toll is. **Preparation is a must for all "do not get mad, get even" ventures.** No preparation means your only option is to get mad. No getting even.

When handing him the package, the reaction is predictable: That guy is going to say "hand me the money, you cannot pay in toffees". Tell him you can. Argue mildly. The traffic held behind will amplify the heat – not to worry. To escalate the situation, have your confederate walk over to the other toll stations and hand over to other drivers, similar bags of toffees. They will instantly catch on. If you have organized this properly at ten stations during peak hour at, say, the Gurgaon Toll road or the Worli Sea-link you will have the grandest example of how getting even, not mad works.

Never get mad. Get even.

---

[48] Rupee (A Rupee/s is abbreviated as Rs.) Roughly Equal to about 0.6 cents.

Once upon a time in Orissa

A tale that unravels why things work when they don't!!!! And vice-versa…

Once upon a time in Orissa[49] there was a big-time police inspector called Inspector Dash. He had a big *Mucchi*[50] and a big "goan"[51]. There was another big-time police inspector called inspector Pattanaik. He had an even bigger *Mucchi* and a much bigger "goan".

Now as things would have it, Inspector Dash wanted to send Inspector Pattanaik a secret message. It was sooooo secret that even he couldn't quite say what it was. However, it went something like this "Manmath Kundu is **pushing** the **bus".**

[49] Orissa is a Big State in India with a huge repertoire of Wildlife, Culture and Natural resources.

[50] *Mucchi* is colloquial for Moustache. In some cultures, the bigger the moustache, the more the wearer is to be respected.

[51] 'Goan' is a local way of pronouncing Gun!

Why this is a secret message and what its tantalizing import is, is not important here. What is important and vexing here is the fact that in spite of his big *Mucchi* and big 'goan', Inspector Dash could simply not send the secret message to Inspector Pattanaik. And the reason was very clear.

Orissa is a coastal state and it had recently been hit by a cyclone. Inspector Dash picked up the phone – it was not working. Inspector Dash switched on the computer – it was not working (no electricity). The police radio was not working. Internet – it was not working. Cell phone- it was not working. He tried sending his messenger by motorcycle -all the roads were flooded. Post office – not working. Courier – not working. Railways – not working. Even by normal standards, this was an extraordinary level of NOT WORKING.

Now, what was poor Inspector Dash to do? His *Mucchi* was already drooping and his 'goan' barrel was beginning to bend from all its master's frustration. In utter desperation he picked up the NGO directory for Bhubhaneshwar – it has thousands of NGOs[52], to see if any NON-Government thing was working!!!!! He dialed one, then the second and then the third. He used his big voice and big *mucchi* and waggled his big 'goan' around. It was no use. All the NGOs refused to help – not that they could have helped to get his secret message across to Inspector Pattanaik. To the last thousand they said the same thing:

[52] NGOS are Non-Governmental Organizations. India has, at last count, some 3,100,000, yes, NGOs, double the number of schools and 250 times the number of Government hospitals!!!!! The Indian Express, August 1, 2015. There is one NGO for 400 people vs. one policeman for 709!

- We help all downtrodden people
- You are NOT downtrodden yet
- Besides you are Government
- We work only for NON-GOVERNMENT folks

And then an idea flew into Inspector Dash's mind. The Orissa police had some birds, very special birds. Purebred carrier pigeons, they were the postmen of the air. And the Orissa police had a bunch of them. They were world-famous.

Off went Inspector Dash's 'gofer[53]' Constable Mohapatra to the pigeon cages with Inspector Dash's secret message. He chose the Balasore pigeon because Inspector Pattanaik lived in Balasore. He attached the message to a band on the carrier pigeon's leg and off it flew. In two hours this astonishingly fast bird had covered the 200 km to Balasore and landed on Inspector Pattanaik's desk. He gingerly picked the message off the bird's leg band and read the message. At last, he knew that "Manmath Kundu is **pushing** the **bus"!!!!!!!!!** He was now at peace and his *Mucchi* was sprightlier than ever.

A few days later the Orissa Government retired the Carrier Pigeon department. No one knows what happened to the Birds.

NOTE: In March 2002, it was announced that India's Police Pigeon Service messenger system in Orissa was to be retired, due to the expanded use of the Internet.

http://news.bbc.co.uk/2/hi/south_asia/1892085.stm

---

[53] 'gofer' is slang for a person who runs errands- 'go for' this and 'go for 'that!

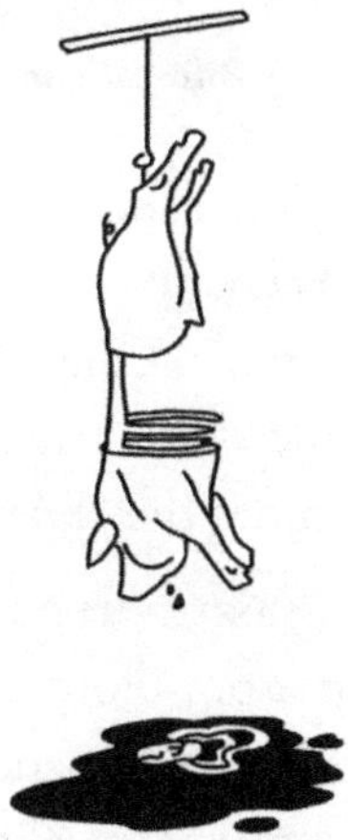

People Simply Love Animals

Warning – Extreme Content

The environmental NGOs had it that all was different now and that people simply loved animals, all of them. And Governments met regularly at all sorts of international conferences to prove and shout again that "EVERYONELOVESANIMALS". And posters and movies and labels, water bottles, soft toys, windcheaters and T-Shirts, school bags and badges all said _ PEOPLE LOVE ANIMALS. Every one of them, without exception. Cute and cuddly as the Panda and downwards. People had changed and now they simply bled for the animals and loved them to bits.

And all the animals cheered. They came out of their holes and burrows, warrens and hutches, nests and tunnels, from the sky, earth, water, and all places in between to celebrate. Their greatest enemy had forsworn battle and now was in love with them. And they had a great big to-do.

With dancing and thumping, and howling and shrieking: dawn, day, dusk and night. Now life would be so much simpler. Only fangs and jaws, speed and stealth, camouflage and skill, venom and sharp senses would count. These were things they knew how to work with.

No more guns, bows and arrows, harpoons, traps, snares, poison, blow darts, electricity, explosives, nets, hooks and all things made of plastic, steel, wire, sinew and human cunning they knew not how to counter. And so the animals rejoiced at the end of all this.

But there were a few who wondered. The great horned owls, awesome Grey Wolf Packs thinking Barramundi, honey badgers- the bravest of them all, the old old elephants, the playful dolphins, and otters.... Some of them wondered – can it really be true? Could humans have changed so much? Was it a BIG LIE? After all, humans had murdered on a scale even disease and nature couldn't. Humongous American Buffalo herds, now down to a few hundred, passenger pigeon flocks that darkened American Skies – now ALL gone, Thylacine, DODOs, all gone. Mahogany almost extinct, Baobabs – *Adansonia grandidieri*, almost gone. How could they trust this species, the humans? Only what fed them, clothed them, warmed them, made shoes and laid eggs were safe. Or got them money in zoos and circuses. All else had always been fair game. Actually unfair game.

And so they asked the big-time animal cootchie-pootchie groups. And all the groups pointed out big fat campaigns. No fur. Beauty without cruelty. Dolphin safe. Save the Habitat, Save the Whale Shark, Save the Snow Leopard, Save the Orangutan. Save the pointy-nosed, great carbuncle encrusted crested serpent fish or some such. Funny how all these campaigns focused on what was almost gone.........

But then the gang, the owl, dolphin, elephant, grey wolf, honey badger, barramundi and otter together with the crow were not quite sure. So they asked their old friends Bila and Kabun to help.

When they did, Bila and Kabun told them it was not a smart idea to ask such questions. They said that some questions are pregnant with unwanted answers. But the gang said they really wanted to know whether humans had changed. So Bila and Kabun said, "so be it".

So what did Bila and Kabun show the gang? They didn't tell them anything. They merely showed them. And left it to the gang to figure out for themselves. They wore helmet-mounted secret cameras and hooked up a sat-nav connected monitor in the forest for the gang to see.

And they went to a stationery shop. To buy some pencils and brushes. Amongst other brushes, there were ones made of camel hair, Siberian weasel tail and boar bristles.

And then they showed them the TV shows where people ate exotic foods for fun: fertilized eggs about to hatch, scorpions, blow-torched marmots, guinea pigs, lizards, caterpillars, grubs and beetles, and spiders.

Unborn fish eggs from the grand Caspian sturgeon: Beluga, Sevruga, Osetra, were prized for flavor – caviar. No babies. And the sturgeon takes 45 years to mature – to be able to make eggs that can give babies....

Ivory from Narwhal and Elephant were banned and so even more valuable.

People from all over the world hunted whales, seals, dolphins, sea lions, penguins, and polar bear under the PROTECTION of one law or another. For fur, skin, bone and skin. The most prized were the baby seals killed in their mother's wombs, they yielded the softest fur of all.

Salmon and geese, migrating thousands of kilometers to spawn and lay eggs were caught for food and shot and fished for sport.

Entire forests that were home to trees, plants, shrubs, grasses, sedges, creepers and moss, home to thousands of insects, spiders, mammals, birds, reptiles, amphibians were burnt, razed and cleared to plant a few crops. Every day more and more land was taken up for every imaginable, THEIR, activity. Roads, dams, houses, ports and everything else killed, denied and drove away all forms of life except THEIRS.

Rivers and lakes were dammed, poisoned and drained till they gave up.

Pesticides, fungicides, herbicides and insecticides killed friends and foes. The ones THEY didn't want were killed as well as the praying mantises, ladybugs and dragonflies who were friends. The birds who ate these tainted insects died as well.

For "medicine" THEY killed rhino for their horn, tigers for their claws and testicles, bears for their paws and gall bladders and lizards and birds, shrubs and roots by the millions. To test their other 'allopathic' medicines they blinded, maimed, lacerated, injected, cut and bled beagles, rats, guinea pigs and sometimes even their own.

They bred kangaroo, emu, crocodile and rhea for their meat and fur. Buffalo, cow, sheep, goat, pig, vicuna, duck, and hen, all bred for food. The mighty seafaring salmon and ballet dancing trout were confined to piddly cages in fish farms. Playful elephant kids were bullied by massive "*kumkis*[54]" and bludgeoned into submission to serve the worship of their gods and to work lumber.

THEY could multiply indefinitely but kangaroos, giraffe, elephant all had to be "culled"

Anyone who ate, what THEY liked was game: coyote, wolf, kea, shark....

Bears, elephants, lions, tigers, parrots, monkeys, chimpanzees, and even incredible dolphins and massive killer whales were made to play THEIR kinds of games in circuses – mere toys. Some they kept at home bred beyond all recognition. Magnificent wolves had been bred to just shadows: dogs, some with their tails docked and some with their vocal cords cut so they wouldn't bark.

They created oases in the middle of deserts and fenced them with electricity so no one else could drink water.

They liked just some parts so they took them and threw the rest away to die agonizing, painful, long-drawn-out deaths: frogs with their legs cut off, sharks with their fins sliced off and thrown back into the sea.

They watched those in their power before eating them: frogs, lobsters, crabs, and fish in tanks waiting for death to

---

[54] "(Kumkis are super trained elephants that in concert, help subdue and train other elephants).

relieve them, dying a thousand times before one of 'them' chose, in a restaurant.

They stole milk from infant cows and buffaloes, venom from snakes, wool from sheep, camel and vicuna, fruit from trees, roots from shrubs, flowers from plants and vines, seeds, pods, grain and leaves. THEY stole the noses from dogs to help hunt for explosives, narcotics, contraband and their lost people.

In the name of religion, ceremony and ritual, they plucked feathers from magnificent birds of paradise and peacocks. They fished the seas with nets so fine, most of the catch could only be used as fertilizer. They killed thousand-year coral to make baubles and trinkets. Tossed in dynamite for a few fish. They robbed birds who had no building material and so used their saliva-the swifts, for bird's nest soup and even the honey from bees who made it one tiny droplet at a time.

Horses, buffalo, camel and dog to pull, lift, shift and travel. To hunt, explore, pillage and lay waste....Nothing was sacred, nothing that lived or died in the Air, Land or water was safe.

Even the paper they used to spread pamphlets and posters to save the animals used more paper from more forests...... Nothing was sacred, nothing that lived in the Air, Land or water was safe. Not even thoughts in the minds or feelings in the heart......nothing could be trusted.

The transmission suddenly stopped. And the gang knew why. They hid the sat nav –monitor in the bushes. And then the whole forest and two of THEM cried themselves to sleep.

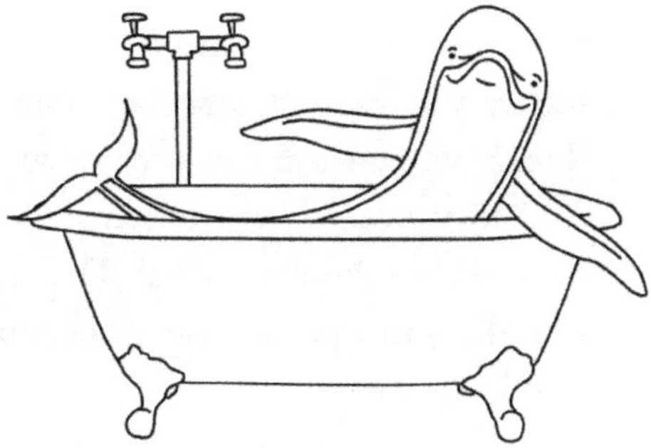

Pets Unlimited

A Kolaa Raoo (MBA) Story

Another Kolaa Raoo story!!!!!

Kolaa Raoo was an MBA. In Gujarati, they call it "*Mane Baddhu Aavdeche*"[55]. And Kolaa Raoo had read tons of theory. He had also 'solved' megatons of cases in B-School. Never mind whether they worked in real life – he had done them in the classroom and surely they would work in real life as well – or so went the theory that Kolaa Raoo and millions of MBAs so fervently believed.

Kolaa Raoo worked for a TRIPS company. Traditionally Run Indian Private Sector Companies are those that have grown over the years and are run traditionally. A few of them in an urge to modernize had started recruiting MBAs to run some of their business. Mind you, not the big-time stuff -just the Chhota mota[56] stuff. And the one that Kolaa Raoo worked for – the Sethji-Malikji Company was in a

[55] I know everything

[56] Small, tiny stuff

hurry to look good. And they found that the flavor of the season was to start a school. Lots of TRIPS were doing that. Set up a trust, run a school and begin to look good!!!!! And they needed someone to run it. And so Kolaa Raoo became the school principal. This freshly minted MBA now was the principal of the Ancientben – Hoarypast-Sethji Malikji School.

So he took charge and as MBAs are wont to do, took an immediate interest in what he knew the least about. He could have worked on the following:

- Smooth school bus service
- A clean dry school in the rains
- Good furniture
- A well-run school textbook-stationery store
- A clean mess
- A nice room for teachers to meet and have tea
- Flowers in the lawns
- Good labs and a solid computer lab
- Good child safety around the school.

But no. He didn't. All these he could have addressed with his common sense and his education. But he didn't. He chose to address students' psychological affiliations.

He happened to have read some Reader's Digest articles. One was on how children spend more time on video games and social networking sites which may not be a great thing. The other one was on how pets can engage the elderly, the lonely, and foster feelings of friendship and caring.

For reasons that are not clear at the moment, Kolaa Raoo mixed these two articles up, in addition to other things and insisted he had read this mishmash in the Journal of School Management – apparently a source of iron-clad, research-based, totally trustworthy information. So his idea was now crystal clear – children will become more social and confident if they have pets and besides will do better at their studies. And he reasoned that if he could implement this in his school, he would steal a march over the other Antiqueben-prehistoricbhai-Lalaji-Sahukar school across the road.

And so with a clear conscience and even clearer intent he strode into the hallowed portals of the Ancientben – Hoarypast-Sethji Malikji School on Monday morning. 'Children-pet compulsory' was his anthem. Naturally, he had made a Wikipedia assisted list of pets. One child – one pet, he declared. In his eagerness to get his totally muddled idea implemented, he completely overlooked two things: children and types of pets and also the dangers of a blindly copy-pasted (as MBAs do for their projects) pet list from Wikipedia.

To monitor the success of his PET-pet-project, as he grandly called it he set up a huge numerical chart. It was a humongous chart full of attendance, time, date, choice of pet, progress of the pet, progress of the child, child's sociability index, child's marks- subject-wise, pet's marks subject-wise......oops we are getting carried away here!!! Kolaa Raoo was so fond of the chart that he briefly contemplated NOT allowing anyone to write anything on it, but that would be soooo silly.

So he announced his project, told the teachers that all students must fill up their choices by that afternoon. They should acquire their pets immediately. And by the end of the week, he wanted students to show grade improvement and complete disgust with social networking sites. And to add spice and zest to it, he made it a secret project. Kids were not to tell their parents but raise their pets secretly!!!!

That day there was normal attendance in school. The next day it fell a bit. And for every day of the week attendance fell little by little. And something curious was happening. Of the few children who did come in, many seemed to be injured. And the next week there were hardly any children coming to school. Kolaa Raoo was astonished.

You see the kids coming to school were the ones who had chosen cat, dog, rabbit, guinea pig, hamster, duck, and chicken. See what had happened to the slower ones since they had to choose the other animals on the list as pets.

Anamika had ticked Python. She got home a python. And now the python had wound one end around the bedpost along with Anamika and was demanding a deer for breakfast and would not let go.

Bhishan and Charu had got porpoise. This one was now in their bathtub upstairs. Now porpoises grow very fast and to do that they need loads of food – fresh fish. And so Bhishan and Charu were working day and night to feed it and did not have the time to go to school. Besides the porpoise had grown in a week and its tail was now outside their bathtub. Their parents were mystified as to why their children were taking week-long baths and hardly ever came out of the bathroom.

Dhruv had got Wooly Mammoth and was away in Northern Alaska where they were last seen. You see at some point, someone in history must have had a woolly mammoth for a pet (damn Kolaa Raoo).

Esha was under arrest. Her pet was a peacock and since it is a Schedule I protected bird, the Forests Department had asked the police to arrest her and the peacock, which was now frantically pecking her.

Feroze had Giant Panda which being from China had an instruction booklet in Chinese attached, which he was trying to decipher. Meanwhile being Made in China, it was quite shoddy and had the mouth and bumboo interchanged. Feroze was having quite a time trying to find which end to feed.

Garima had Hornbill which had resolutely plastered itself inside a mud wall and now insisted on being fed through a slit.

Hormuz had an albatross which each time it opened its huge, magnificent wings pushed him out of the window.

Imtiaz had a raccoon which was driving him crazy since it wanted water to wash everything.

Jyotsna had a bat that insisted on hanging upside down driving her quite dizzy and besides she could not switch on the ceiling fan for fear of hurting it.

Kashyap had a Polar Bear which insisted on keeping the a/c at such horrifically low temperatures that he was forced to cover himself in six jackets and was having trouble walking.

Lara had a Killer Whale which she was looking after at the municipal swimming pool.

Manipadma had a Great Horned Owl which kept making such dreadful noises that it scared his parents out of their wits.

Naju had a wolf who howled at the moon and was giving everyone in the neighbourhood, wet pajamas.

Outrosh had a Giant Sloth that stank to the heavens and in the whole first week had not finished its potty after going in on the very first day!!!

Piyush and Peepika the twins had a Hoolock Gibbon which insisted on a tree right in their bedroom. When they refused it started howling and yowling so loudly that the twins swung outside their window and begged the *Gulmohar*[57] outside to send a bough in quickly!!!!!!

Quadri had a praying mantis which ate only live mosquitoes and flies.

Rashesh had a scorpion which threatened him with both ends: its vicious stinger and its evil claws. Besides, it had hundreds of babies on its back.

And so the list went, meerkats, tapirs, jaguars, elephants, wildebeest, rhino, dinosaurs, amoeba, plankton, oryx… the list was truly formidable.

The kids were having an impossible time trying to keep their pets alive while being bitten, clawed, nipped, scratched, kicked, gored and generally scared to death.

The most amazing part was that to make sure they did the right thing by their pets, they had to ask around: friends, experts, wild-lifers, biologists and everyone else. They also needed money to buy food. So they asked friends and other

---

[57] A type of tree

supporters. And they did all this by social networking!!!!!! Facebook, Twitter and so on full time!!!!!!!!

By the next Monday, Kolaa Raoo was fed up with the poor attendance and sent a stinker of a letter to all absent students. Better come next Monday or we will strike you off our rolls he threatened. This made the kids sooooo angry, they decided to teach Kolaa Raoo a lesson. So they used Facebook, Twitter and Instagram to organize a big to-do!!!!

On Monday when Kolaa Raoo sat down in his office, his secretary said that the students had invited him to the assembly in the auditorium. When he got into the auditorium it was all dark. And there was a strange smell all around. Suddenly the door shut behind him and then the lights went on. And what he saw was like 1000 years of the National Geographic magazine had been cut and pasted into one gigantic POSTER.

Animals, birds, reptiles, insects, spiders, fishes….. all glaring at him. And holding each one of them, his students. His mouth opened wide, his jaw dropped and he just had time to hear ALL his students shouting at their pets: "GO GET HIM"…. And chased by a rhino, gibbon, chimpanzee, defective panda, scorpion, wasp, python…… and 500 hundred students, Kolaa Raoo just managed to get the door open. Last seen he was running down the highway as fast as his legs would carry him, his shirt gone, his pant torn and his zebra-striped *chuddy*[58] flapping in the wind.

And then the kids sent all the animals to the zoo and then all lived happily ever after.

---

[58] (underwear)

Ratios not Quite in Proportion!!!

Sher Singh[59] and *Badmash Singh*[60] were two tiger brothers. They were young, ultra-fit and very, very strong. And they were super smart. Sometimes it appeared that they had one and half brains each instead of the usual one per tiger!!!

They had all the tigerish qualities: sharp claws, pointy teeth with strong jaws to match, super hearing, fantastic eyesight and an incredible sense of smell. They were true masters of the jungle. They strutted around proudly and every animal was totally scared of them. They killed and ate when hungry and generally lazed around the whole day. In winter, in sunny meadows, sprawled with all legs in the air. In summer it would be in one of the cool streams that flowed through the jungle.

They loved to be photographed and would sashay around in magnificent poses whenever those touristy photographers

[59] *Sher* means Lion. *Singh* too means lion; a popular surname Therefore *Sher Singh* is one hell of a name. Technically a Tiger is a *Babbar Sher.*

[60] Badmash Means 'naughty or mischievous'

came around on elephants, jeeps or whatever. Sometimes they would open up their maws to show off pointy fangs. Other times they would crouch low behind some far away deer as if in the pre-attack mode. This would lead to much oohs and aahs and clicky, clicky clackety, clicky photos. Once a small kid with a crappy camera was trying to get some good shots. It was obvious his camera was not up to the job. *Sher Singh* and *Badmash Singh* got closer and closer to the kid. They were just trying to help. *Badmash Singh* was combing his magnificent whiskers with his claws for better effect. But they had got too close and the kid was so frightened he pissed in his pants and bawled for his mother and generally everyone in their jeep got jittery.

Since then they kept their distance and didn't do anything that would scare off people. If it was one of those arty-farty wildlife photographers.... Oh but that is another story.

But what they liked best was reading. Well actually being read to. Yes. And whenever Bila and Kabun would camp in the forest, *Sher Singh* and *Badmash Singh* would be on their best behavior and land up at camp. Then they would hunker down and wait till Bila and Kabun were free and ask them to read. All sorts of stuff. But the ones they liked best was "ghost stories". Hey, not the ghouls and banshees and vampires and that kind of stuff. Wildlife stories. "The Man-eaters of Kumaon" by Jim Corbett[61], a famed Man-eating Tiger hunter was what sent shivers along their spines,

---

[61] The Man-eaters of Kumaon by Jim Corbett, an iconic book that has defined many a life path – this author included. A legendary hunter, especially of man-eating tigers, his courage, skill, and storytelling are of the highest order.

down their long tails and then racing back to their heads and then the shivers sat on top of their pointy ears for days. In fact, they found these stories so scary that if they had a bit of a constipation problem, they just had to remember "Jim Corbett"!

They liked these stories. And as the stories were read by the campfire, *Sher Singh* and *Badmash Singh* would inch closer to each other and then to Bila and Kabun till things got a little 'Amusing' or 'Frightening'; depending on the way you looked at it. Amusing because two great BIG HULKING tigers in their prime were sidling up to two small kids because they, the tigers, were frightened. Frightening because two great BIG HULKING F R I G H T E N E D tigers in their prime with claws, paws and incredible power were right next to two small kids.

Now it so happened one day that Bila and Kabun kept working and working and hadn't read any stories to them at all. So *Sher Singh* and *Badmash Singh* waited and waited and waited – no story in sight, er, sound, er... you know what I mean. And so they edged closer and closer till Kabun jumped up when a bunch of whiskers obscured her notebook. 'Sorry' said *Sher Singh* from one side and *Badmash Singh* from the other. They were just trying to read what she was doing. Both Kabun and Bila threw down their books in disgust. "oh, it is all these Ratios and Proportions[62]... such dreadfully boring stuff" they sighed in unison. "Please

---

[62] An important mathematical concept. It is taught at most schools in a way that miraculously manages to be confusing, boring, sexist and impractical at the same time. The usual contexts include men and women digging wells, constructing walls or mixing liquids – none of which are of the remotest interest to any normal schoolchild.

tell us ratios and proportions story" chimed *Sher Singh* and *Badmash Singh*. Obviously, they thought it was some kind of story for they had never been to school.

And so Bila and Kabun exchanged glances and then told them. If one man can build a wall in 17 days and one woman can build a wall in 25; in how many days can three women and 7 men build the wall? Four huge blank, bewildered eyes flanked by quivering whiskers stared back at them. If one man equals three women and it takes 17 men and X women 16 days to dig a well, then how many women were in the well? Now the tiger's ears were quivering as well. They began shivering ever so slightly and sidling up towards Bila and Kabun.

Astonished they asked the tigers what was up? And the tigers said OK they built a wall, and then a well and now some trapping is going to happen no? "Silly Goose, well Geese" shouted Bila and Kabun. You just don't understand… Well, neither do we, this is boring. And just to get the tigers off their laps they explained how it worked. Fat lot of good it did. Because by the time they finished, both the tigers were snoring loudly, heads in their laps and legs curled around them. Bila and Kabun helped each other push the monsters off their laps and then slept on top of a very warm, furry living bed!!!![63]

In the morning the tigers went off in search of food. A passing hare saw them and was so frightened that it leaped

[63] Dingoes are the endemic wild dogs of Australia. Aborigines, the indigenous people to whom Australia belonged, use an ingenious measurement of temperature. A five dingo night is pretty cold for it takes that many dingoes as living blankets to stay warm!

straight into the air. *Sher Singh* roared, just for fun, and a poor boa constrictor on the treetop lost her hold and fell. And suddenly *Sher Singh* said to *Badmash Singh*: "hey look if one tiger with one roar can frighten so much, how much will two tigers be able to frighten". "Aha, said *Badmash Singh*, if one tiger with two eyes can see kilometers into the forest, how far can four tiger eyes see". And in this way, they were soon adding up claws, paws, ears, noses, teeth, and tails and finally decided that, with their understanding of math, there definitely was scope for a METAtiger with 'eleventy-eleven' more power than just one tiger.

Now how do you test such wonderful tiger math? And so *Badmash Singh* thought and thought and then came up with an idea only a tiger like him could. "Why do we not hunt elephants?" asked *Badmash Singh* of his brother. So his brother answered, "Coz big males are too big, and the females stick together, and if we even go near the babies, the mothers would kill us... so there". "Exactly," said *Badmash Singh* so that is what we need to do".

"Explain," said *Sher Singh*. And so *Badmash Singh* did. It involved ratios and proportions. They would ambush a BIG male elephant from both sides. Hopefully a lone male in '*Musth*[64]' who would be even more bad-tempered. Then all of a sudden, at a signal from *Badmash Singh*, both would roar horrendously and leap onto the elephant's back. And then ratio and proportions would work.

---

[64] *Musth* – A bull elephant condition with super high hormonal levels and super aggressive behavior towards all other animals. The word '*Musth*' is from the Persian and is often used colloquially for people in a much milder reference.

Poor *Sher Singh* didn't understand a word of this but didn't want to look as if he didn't understand math, so he went along with *Badmash Singh*.

So they trailed and ambushed a lone BIG male elephant as per plan, roared and jumped on his back. The massive elephant promptly trumpeted, whacked his trunk around and rolled over on his back.

When the dust had cleared, there was an extraordinary-looking creature standing on the forest floor. It had two mouths, four ears, two noses, four eyes, eight legs, and two tails. When it tried to flick one tail, it got entangled in the other one and couldn't do much. When it tried to walk, the eight legs couldn't quite coordinate and in the end, it had to move in a droopy wavy motion, much like a caterpillar. The eyes were focused in all directions and together looked more like a security camera than a fierce METAtiger. The combined roar was more like a squeak since the roars we out of phase and cancelled each other.

And slowly, all the animals of the forest came to see this fantastic creature. The fox shook his head, the pheasants giggled, the squirrel babies ran on its back and used its tails as a sort of slide. And things came to a pretty pass when the owl sat on its heads, one foot on each head and announced to the whole forest that this new animal was a freak of nature, was to be treated as a guest and all animals should be kind to it!!!!!!!

And then the fearless honey badger asked the animal what kind of animal it was......"*BadmashSherSingh*"... came the squeaky reply!!! All the animals started laughing. All tiger parts of the METAtiger felt miserable. Bila and

Kabun too felt horrible. But what were they to do? They knew school math is stupid, but they never knew it was this bad.

So they decided to do their holiday homework and then in the evening see what they could do for *BadmashSherSingh*. And so they discussed their latest nuisance of a problem in Ratio and Proportions. Suppose 3 men can lay a Carpet for the *Sahib*[65] in 4 days and 7 women can lay the same Carpet for the *Sahib* in 11 then how many men and women can lay the Carpet for the *Sahib* in just 1 day….oh what a big bore….come-on why don't we just shoot this thing down …and help *BadmashSherSingh* instead?

And poor *BadmashSherSingh* overheard them. But because all their four ears were pointing this way and that, up and down, left and right, this is what it heard. "Men….. Carpet *Sahib*……in One day….Big Bore……Carpet *Sahib*. Shoot……Kumaon(come-on)…*BadmashSherSingh*".

And then all hell broke loose. Humongous shivering, shaking, jumping, pulling, pushing, shake, shudder, wobble, waggle, wiggle and then with one gigantic grunt – Badmash*Sher Singh* separated into *Sher Singh* and *Badmash Singh*. And the two tigers raced away in the dark, faster than lightning and were not seen for months afterward..

Was it that they were mortally afraid of Ratios and Proportions now? Well yes, but that's not the whole story. You see Jim Corbett was also affectionately known by the Villagers of Kumaon as 'Carpet *Sahib*'!!!!!

---

[65] *Sahib* – from the Arabic. Means 'Owner". A term of address like "Mister". A term of huge respect.

Shaving the Environment

A primer on why do-gooders are sometimes a pain.

Once upon a time, there was an NGO. Now for those who do not know, an NGO is a Non-Governmental Organization. This is fascinating if you spend some time thinking about it.

Suppose your name is Farokh and someone asks you "What's your name?" Why on earth would you want to reply "I am not Firdaus or Freny or Fatima"?

Again suppose you met a beaver in a forest and you had never seen a beaver before and you asked it "What kind of animal are you?" And the beaver said, "I am not a crocodile". You might say "I can see that you are not a crocodile considering you do not have a huge snout full of razor-sharp teeth". "But what are you?" And the beaver said,

"I am not a giant three-toed sloth". I mean you would think that the animal had gone postal[66].

And so if you ask an NGO what they are, they would tell you we are a Non-Governmental Organization. Ok so you are Non-Government but what ARE you: "a Non-Governmental Organization"!!!! What would you think?????

And there are heaps and hordes of them working/lobbying on problems you never even existed like wildlife trade, obscure plant, insect, fish species, land rights, water rights, air quality, alternate energy, for nuclear power, against nuclear power. NGOs set up for opposing just ONE element of the periodic table – Carbon. NGOs for rocks in the middle of nowhere. Children's rights, adult rights, senior citizens' rights, women's rights, gay rights. In fact, just about anything on planet earth and even beyond. There is actually one for disarmament and peace in outer space!!!!! At some point, you begin to wonder whether Governments do any work at all considering how many NGOs it takes to keep the planet ticking.

And some of the most astonishing ones are in Environment, especially wildlife. City slickers with their best experience of wildlife being, the lizard in their kitchen, infest these NGOs, many of which are in wildlife education. Make no mistake. These NGOs will never educate judges, bureaucrats, politicians, police, armed forces, business people, the National Parks Department, farmers or anyone who could remotely help conserve wildlife and its habitat. They do not, they cannot. If they even tried they would get their asses kicked to hell. So

---

[66] A very different way of saying 'mental'.

they choose the softest of targets: children. And even with children; only those who have time to waste: primary and secondary school kids.

So these poor little kids, NONE of whom are responsible for hunting, poaching, trading in animal parts or habitat destruction are hauled off to the nearest -distant[67], verdant wildlife habitat. There they are taught to save the tiger, snow leopard, whale shark, river dolphin or whatever is the flavor of the day. A week later these kids are back in school with the god-awfulest mixed up notions of environment matched only by a fierce determination to save the slithering talon honeybee or the great flying elephant mole.

And so the kids' group from the Ancientben – Hoarypast-Sethji Malikji School were at the BhitarPutra Dhadhakedar National Park[68] for a Nature Education Camp. It was being conducted by the Society Against Wildlife Habitat Destruction And for Nelson Mandela – SAWDHAN. This is the NGO standard - Sanskrit word expanded into an English name. They badly needed an 'N' at the end of their name, you cannot just call it SAWDHA. So they just put a Nelson Mandela at the end!!!!!

The first day and night were devoted entirely to repeated washing of pants and shorts. You see these city kids' experience of plants and trees was mainly the potted palms in the shopping mall and the crappy Independence day potted plants at school. The dense forest and the noises in

---

[67] As in "which is the nearest place we can feel we are away from the city?"

[68] Hypothetical National Park, but has a nice powerful, rhyming ring to it no?

the dark night….. came as a mega shock expressed in their pants and shorts!!!!! Hence the washing…

The whole of the next day was full of "volunteers" and "Resource Persons". These are code-words that basically mean 'free workers' and 'clueless except in a paralyzingly narrow context". They filled the kids' time and heads with pollution, non-biodegradable plastics, species extinction, resource scarcity (water, wood, food etc..), loss of cultural and natural habitat, the end of fossil fuel, evils of dams, the virtues of vegetarianism, the shrinking ozone layer, global warming and so on. And then there was trekking and walking and the food was not so good but they were hungry. And of course there was a campfire and some songs and more speeches on the horrors visited upon the environment…. And four days later they were back home…

And then the hassles began. Dhruv's mummy went to the kitchen with some bug spray and got an earful. "don't you know pesticides are harmful?". Anisha's mummy saw her weeping at the table – for a boiled egg. Porus would not brush his teeth because the toothbrush was made of plastic. Piyush was trying to push the refrigerator out of the balcony – it contained CFC he insisted and would damage the ozone layer. Salim and Sonam refused to go to school since the bus used diesel and besides it did belch smoke. The kids made up a Facebook gang and refused to have baths to save water. They would not do homework since it would use up paper and as we all know, paper comes from wood, from trees. No pencils for the same reason and besides pencils contain graphite – carbon is a max villain. They wouldn't drink milk since it was 'stolen' from cows' babies and besides the milk came in plastic packets – animal rights and non-biodegradable!!! They wouldn't even breathe hard since it would mean using up more oxygen. They remembered all their resource persons and volunteer's lectures well and made their parents' life hell.

And so the parents got together and asked PICS dad what to do. And so he made the plan for them. The next day, all the parents of all the kids in the

- Ancientben – Hoarypast-Sethji Malikji School
- Who had gone to the wretched Nature Education Camp
- At the BhitarPutra Dhadhakedar National Park
- Conducted by the cursed Society Against Wildlife Destruction Habitat And Nelson Mandela – SAWDHAN formed an association: PATOKPNNGOOTBA, never mind it wasn't Sanskrit and never mind it didn't rhyme. It meant Parents Association To Kick Pesky Nature NGOs On Their Backsides!!

And so advised by PICSdad, the PATOKPNNGOOTBA kicked off[69] their campaign. They told their kids that they had become very environment and nature conscious too. So they agreed with their kids completely and said that they wanted to "Save the Tiger and the Dingbat and the Great Pesky Green Assed Metropole or whatever" and even more. And here was their list for even greater nature redemption:

---

[69] Pun intended

A. No more computers: games, Facebook, email since computers are made of plastic and use electricity from dams.

B. No more pizzas since they contain cheese made from milk stolen from cows.

C. No more fizzy drinks since they contain CARBON – dioxide!!!!

D. No more movies since the animation is done in third world sweatshops.

E. No more iPod/music etc. since they contribute to micro-noise pollution.

F. No more clothes since they are made from plant fiber and as everyone knows, cotton needs need humongous amounts of water to grow.

G. No more yak yakking with friends, for sound is dissipated as heat and can contribute to global warming.

H. No more pets since they are artificially bred.

I. Cockroaches, mice, flies, mosquitoes encouraged to breed in the house, kitchen, bathroom, especially bedbugs in bed – they are wildlife too…

J. No more cell phones since their r/f[70] transmissions cause r/f pollution.

K. Pee Pee and potty in the garden to encourage bio-conversion to compost. No water to be used either – to save water.

---

[70] Radio Frequency

L. Do's

a. Only *khadi* [71]to be worn
b. Silence all-day
c. Only satvik[72] food – *khichdi*[73] and raw *karela*[74] salad
d. Only music allowed – *bhajans*[75]
e. Only clean cut hairstyles allowed
f. Get up at the crack of dawn and sleep at sunset to conserve electricity.
g. All conversation only in Sanskrit to preserve the culture and prevent cultural pollution

Guess what happened>>>!!! Game, set and match point to PATOKPNNGOOTBA. All lived happily ever after….

---

[71] A type of handspun, coarse cotton cloth inextricably linked with Mahatma Gandhi and the Indian Nationalist spirit.

[72] Holy and ultra-healthy

[73] An ultra-basic food with just boiled rice and lentils

[74] Bitter Gourd

[75] Religious Chants

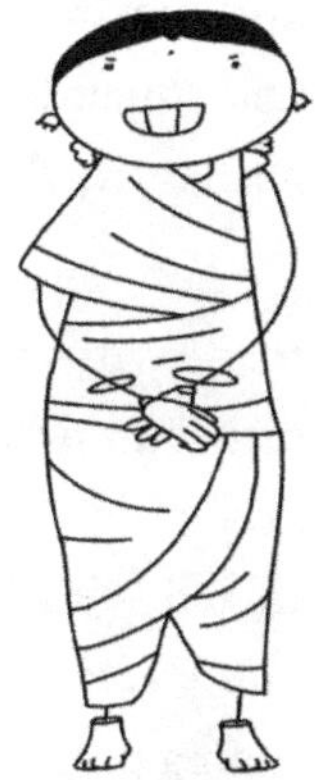

Vampire' s Authentic South Indian Restaurant[76]

She was fed up. Not fed well, just fed up. With all the crap that masqueraded in the name of South Indian food. The '*Yidli*' in 60 flavors, the '*Dhonsa*' in 200 including chicken and fish. She was pissed off with the watery, sweet, diarrheal mess with a few pumpkin floating around called '*Somebhar*' and the useless mush full of peanuts they euphemistically named "*Chutney*". She was fed up with the sick orange-colored mess that passed for tomato *chutney*. She was sick of the pulverized disaster they called, of all the things: 'gunpowder'. Thoroughly disgusted. She wandered

[76] This is a deep context story. It needs in-depth knowledge of a particular cuisine. In another sense, it delivers knowledge and the desire to know, of a particular cuisine. The argument is very simple. If one knows quesadillas, risottos, teppanyaki and 'Gopi Majurian', why the hell should they not know something deeply Indian? **Learn**, you miserable 'foodies'!

and meandered in search of some 'real' stuff. She wandered and squandered her taste buds to no avail. The original, the authentic, the real McCoy was nowhere to be found.

For VAMPire thought of Industrial Strength *Sambar* made with small onions, sizzling coconut *chatni* with crisply sautéed curry leaf floating on top. And of course the one and only *Molagapodi*, the real one with horse gram and mixed with sesame/gingelly oil. And with it would be the *dosai, elai-adai, veriverishi adai, pesarattu*, giant *idlies* softer than a politician's spine, crisp *dosai* and venturing deep into the South Indian psyche and panache: *aapam, idi-appam, kozhakattai (ammini, uland* and *birangi*), *puttu, sevai, neer* and set *dosais*!!!!!! Oh wow, where were they? Would she have to resign herself forever to these shady imposters: The *Uthappams* and *Dhonsas*, the counterfeit, the masqueraders, the fakes, pretenders????

Dripping and mouth-watering VAMPire though and though. She felt pity for the ignorant masses eating the trash available. What would they say to a classic *Aapam* with a magnificent *Ishtew*?????

And then she had a brainwave that ran all through her, from her toes to the top of her head. It rushed into her hands till her fingers tingled. She would. Why should she spend time searching? She should do it. Deliver the huddled masses from the tyrants of the phonies. She would do it herself.

Thus was born the VAMPire's AUTHENTIC SOUTH INDIAN Restaurant. Original food for sure including the filter coffee. Even the other stuff, the gods, the *agarbattis*[77],

[77] Incense Sticks

the music, the banana leaves, the upturned coffee glasses resting on their *dawaras*[78]..the works. 100% Authentic South Indian. Restaurant opens at the beginning of the Universe of delights. Breathless anticipation.

And then the UP Man came in and asked for "*Dahi Bada*". Looking at him fiercely VAMPire said to him "o *ji yahan sab bada hai, lekin ham dahi same size banate hain, dahi koh bada kaise banaye*?". UP man went off muttering into his beard.

And then the Gujarati came in. Ordered *idli*. And found the *sambar* too spicy. He asked for some jaggery to make it sweeter. Having got up from the floor where she had fallen, VAMPire, took away his dishes and booted him out.

The *Sardarji* ordered for *Upma*. When the steaming hot dish came to him, he took one bite and started screaming "*Saaala karha parshad mein namak dal diya hai*[79]". VAMPire assumed the Sardar was cursing the cook – Prasad Rao and seeing any way that *Sardar* was unhappy with the food, sent him away.

The came Manmath Kundu. He sat down looked at what the others were eating. The *vadas* seemed tempting. So he called VAMPire, pointed to the table next to him and said: "Too piss *vada*". Enraged by such a brazenly obvious insult to her vadas and obscene behavior, she booted him out of the restaurant.

And then some Army men came in, looked at the Menu and told VAMPire to get the Indian Menu. She looked at

---

[78] Bowls

[79] Rascal has put salt in the votive offering

them flabbergasted. After all, it was an Indian Restaurant and it was INSIDE India. So what was the problem? She explained that a South Indian Restaurant was definitely an Indian restaurant. The Army men stubbornly insisted that they would eat ONLY out of an Indian menu. "Look at this one catering to sedition and anti-national feelings and violating the idea of a country". This really got VAMPire's goat. How in hell could these people say such stuff about her ORIGINAL, AUTHENTIC restaurant? As if it was serving pizzas or pasta or was located in enemy territory. The Army Men pointed out the "Mysore-Pak" in the menu and demanded to know since when had a part of an Indian state declared independence and associated itself with another country. The Indian Army would not tolerate such nonsense and would she please get the Menu which would make them less angry. Soon they were out on the street looking for another restaurant.

And then a bunch of golfers came in. When they got the menu they waved it away and said: "we will eat after the game". So very graciously VAMPire told them to do that. They could enjoy their game and afterward could enjoy her delicious food. So the golfers asked her to clear all the tables and chairs and where was the mini-golf course. And they didn't want to play somewhere else, they wanted to play right there. Astonished, she demanded they explain. See the sign outside your restaurant. It says "today's special – *Puttu*". So we want to practice our *Putts* here. Back to the street, they went.

And some stationery shops and the post office asked if she would like to supply them. Her delight lasted only milliseconds before she realized they had assumed the *morkuzhu* to be adhesive paste!!!!!!!!!!

And the teenagers who wanted to see the comic book in which a Bollywood star made an appearance – *Nellikai Archie-Kalki*!!!!!!! And everyone who turned their coffee-in-*dawarah* upside down and flipped them again not knowing how to take the coffee out. And those who wanted sugar and jaggery to make everything less spicy, people who wanted prawn *dosa*. She had dismissed all her waiters and rehired them as bouncers to kick people out into the street.

The turning point came when one day a family came in. One of those upmarket culture vulture types who barely transit airports around the world and then claim to have in-depth knowledge of that whole country and besides now speak their mother tongue with a foreign accent. Just such a bunch landed up. Father, mother and two kids. When VAMPire came over to their table because she loved kids and wanted them to have an extra good time, she was stopped in her tracks. Much like the wagons slamming into huge, solid concrete walls at the NASA crash test facility. That's exactly how VAMPire was stopped in her tracks. The fury and rage started as a small spark and then grew outwards from her tummy. It spread all over her like a perfect firestorm and erupted as a flaming thermonuclear volcano. The moron culture vulture mother had picked up some of the authentic, oh-so-special *molagapodi* in her fist and was making designs on the banana leaf all the while explaining to her idiot children and husband about how tribal cultures use sand and local materials to create art. The Mexicans did sand drawings and Indians did a similar thing called rangoli and the South Indians did '*Koll-am*' and glanced up at VAMPire to receive compliments at her extensive knowledge of SOUTH INDIAN TRADITION.

The volcano blast spread outwards: "*KOLLAM* is a place in Kerala, *Kolam* is what you should have said but now what I am going to do is to, in Tamil, Kannada, Malayalam and Telugu is to ***Kollam Pohunnu*** – TO KILL you". With that she rushed back to the kitchen to get the biggest ladle she could lay her hands on. The culture vultures vanished.

The restaurant is shut and VAMPire now lives somewhere in the Himalayas she won't reveal.

An OWL Story

Once upon a time, there was a family of snowy owls.1 father, 1 mother and 3 little babies. Now, when the babies grew up, the father decided to teach them hunting.

Then he first took them on to a snowy place where an Arctic Hare was eating. He said, "now I want you to spot your prey without opening your eyes". Then the snowy owl babies closed their eyes and tried to see the arctic hare. Of course, they couldn't. So they opened their eyes and the arctic Hare saw their eyes and ran away. Then the father kicked them on their bumboos.

Then sometime later he took them to a hill. There was another arctic hare. Now he said, "fly up to the arctic hare without flapping your wings". So they jumped off the hill with their wings closed. Of course, they started falling down. So they started flapping their wings to save themselves from falling. The hare heard all this flapping and ran away. Then the father was fed up with them and again kicked all of them soundly on their bumboos.

Now the father owl was an accomplished hunter. So he himself caught an arctic hare. And gave it to his babies. Then he said to the babies "eat without opening your beaks". The babies knew that couldn't do such a thing and immediately lined up for kicks on their bumboos automatically.

Then they went to their house and said to their mother and father "today we will make and feed you dinner". So they laid the table and took some vessels and started to serve make-believe food to their mother and father. The baby owls said, "what are you folks waiting for?" "Eat". So the father said, "where is the food?" The babies said "eat the food without it being there. Just like we are supposed to fly without flapping our wings, eat without opening our beaks and see without opening our eyes". So the father said "Sorry, Sorry. When I told you to see without opening your eyes, I actually meant that open your eyes very little so that the prey cannot see your eyes. Then when I told you to fly without flapping your wings I meant that you should glide and not flap your wings noisily. And when I said to eat without opening your beaks I meant that you should not open your beak, otherwise all the hair will get into your mouth and choke you. You should fist rip open the skin with a closed beak and then start eating when you come to the flesh."

The babies said "OK" and then they made some really nice food and they all had a nice dinner happily.

The Good, the Try to Be Good and The Godly

Goby and Gorl

There once were a boy and a girl who would get up early in the morning in the *Brahma muhurta*[80], brush their teeth and drink an *ayurvedic*[81] potion. We will call then GOOD BOY and GOOD GIRL: GOBY and GORL in short. Then they would do potty. Then they would do some Yoga and then bathe. Then they would pray for a while, drink coffee, eat nutritious dry fruits and a boiled egg. They would dress up in their uniforms which had already been ironed and laid out straight at their desks with belt, tie, socks, polished shoes and all the last night. Their school bags would be packed with the correct books for the next day's classes. Their mom or dad would give them their snack

[80] Ancient texts have it that the hours preceding sunrise are the most auspicious and appropriate for work, learning and meditation

[81] Ancient Indian form of medicine

boxes. Then they would walk to the bus stop taking care to see that they didn't get any dust on their shoes. They would be at least two minutes before time so as not to miss the bus. They would climb in and wish everyone good morning- other children, the driver, teachers and the watchman when they reached the school.

They would then attend the assembly totally in line and very silent. In class, they would wish all their classmates and their teacher very good morning. Then they would extract from their bags, small, small, small steel flat-boxes in which they had packed each subject's text and notebooks. The steel boxes ensured that the text and notebooks would not get dog-eared. And of course three perfectly sharpened pencils per class!!! Whatever the teacher said they would write down in beautiful handwriting, with two carbon copies – one for the teacher as transcript and one to their friends in case they wanted their notes.

After school, straight home where they would put their school clothes to wash, change and then eat a hi-fiber *bajra*[82] roti[83] lunch with lots of salads and vegetables. Sleep precisely for 43 minutes and then go out to jog and do some stretching exercises. Then back home, finish homework, study for another two hours. Then they would pack their bags, set up their uniforms and shoes, etc for the next day. Then dinner, a little *vajrasan*[84] and then off to sleep by ten!!!!!

---

[82] Millet, a super-food

[83] Unleavened Flatbread

[84] A very special post-meal Yoga pose

Tryby and Tryl

GOBY and GORL's neighbors were another boy and girl. These two were trying desperately to be good. Forced by their parents, teachers, relatives and other do-gooders these two were trying so hard, we will call them TRYBY and TRYL. Now, these two were at it full time – how to be good. As good as their model neighbors – GOBY and GORL, maybe, even better. So they wanted to change how they got up, studied, dressed, danced, played, worked, commuted, bathed, were doing the 'in' stuff, eating, singing, …in short – everything. And they were desperate because everyone wanted them to be "GOOD"!!!!

And so one day their parents told them that they must eat one *pudina*[85] leaf and one *neem*[86] leaf in the morning before they went to school. And so TRYBY and TRYL did just that. They were sure one would cleanse their systems and the other would make them alert and smell good!!! Then an uncle advised them that they should drink a glass of Vietnamese Dragon Fruit Juice (VDFJ) every morning as it would help in their studies. VDFJ was helpful in calculus and geography apparently. Diligently, their parents ordered over the internet for it to be delivered to them every morning. So the kids would get up at 5 every morning now to eat *neem* leaf, *pudina* leaf and drink VDFJ. Sensing their weakness in trigonometry and plant biology, the same uncle suggested a small dose of freshly ground cordyceps (I kid you not) from Bhutan every alternate morning. Since poor TRYBY and TRYL were not good at any subject, soon

---

[85] Mint

[86] *Azidarachta Indica*, supposed to have near-magical medicinal qualities

they were getting up at 3 in the morning to receive various courier packages from around the world containing fresh VDF, Cordyceps, Grubs, Beetles, Mangosteen, volcanic ash, edelweiss, Bird guano from Peru, coco-de-mer and suchlike. Their study room was festooned with charts since some of these fruits had to drunk daily, some once in two days, some twice a day, some had to be dripped in the ears and one had to be converted to a paste and put in the belly button. Some chewed, some swallowed some juiced.....Yoga-*Shirshashan*[87] was also recommended as was a glass of hot water. Now their 'get-up' time was 2 a.m. Swami Fraudananda's edict for each responsible citizen to plant a tree a day was conveyed to them by their parents as was the international call for children to save the dolphin. So now they got up even earlier. Save the dolphins – get up at 1.a.m to feed and wash the dolphin in the bathtub. Then the fruit juices, plant a tree, etc, etc. And of course once in a while, mainly due to lack of sleep they would mix things up: drink the dolphin's water and plant trees in the VDFJ while talking to the neem leaf in Parandarese[88]. And of course, if they did *shirsashan* while doing potty, you can imagine the results!!!!

The society pages in the magazines also had it that Parandarese was the language to learn. You see the ambassador of Parandara[89] had been visiting the city and had gently hinted that knowing Parandarese was a way of emigrating to Parandara.

---

[87] Upside down pose that makes blood rush to one's head

[88] Coming up

[89] Hypothetical 'developed' country

So now flat out, TRYBY and TRYL had to get up at 12.00 to include Parandarese in their schedule. One day, their mother's friend showed her an article that said that children were spoiling their backs and their postures by carrying heavy loads to school. So the kids got a brand new wheelbarrow as a present the next day. Now all would know-how up-to-date TRYBY and TRYL's parents were. But the next day, the bus conductor flatly refused to let the wheelbarrow into the bus even if was a cute red color. No building materials on the bus was his rule. TRYL and TRYBY tried explaining that this was a most modern ergonomic-scientific-protonomic-ungostearic[90] method of protecting kid's backs. But the conductor said 'no'. Children in, wheelbarrow out. Or BOTH out. That day TRYL and TRYBY had a bumpy ride to school sitting in the wheelbarrow tied behind the school bus. Their teacher also had a tough time recognizing these two brown, dust-covered figures!! So from the next day, they put the wheelbarrow on top of the school bus. The wheelbarrow business is a long story and that story deserves be told, all by itself. But what it resulted in was a cow they now had to look after in addition to everything else. Their final solution was to live and sleep in the tub: tree plantation, juices, dolphin, potty, yoga and all blub blub bluuuub!!!!!!!

This schedule had its punishments. They progressively got late, missed assignments and fell asleep in class. The dolphin was sick of eating *neem* leaves and the wheelbarrow was a pain to maintain. Sticky fruit juice was all over the place. The lack of sleep resulted in black rings around their

[90] Too new even to have a meaning in place

eyes, making them look like little pandas full of fruits from around the world. They had taken to going to sleep fully clothed in their school uniform with *pudina* leaves in one hand, *neem* in the other, a glass of juice in the third and a tree ready for planting in the fourth. Their toes would be squeezing some fruit while their elbows were massaging the dolphin. And the cow…oh god. They were so tired that they thought it would be a better idea for the dolphin and the cow to go to school instead of them.

Cowboy and Corral

Opposite GOBY AND GORL there lived another boy and girl who always played it cool, so let's call them COWBOY and CORRAL. They would sometimes get up early in the morning and go cycling with their friends or exercise with their mommy. Sometimes they would get up at 12, have breakfast at 1, lunch at 7 and generally go to sleep at 2 in the morning. Once in a while, they would go to school at around 10 in the morning if they could and make it to the second or third class. Notes …hmmm, it would be a miracle if they had taken their school bag itself. One shoe would be a sneaker and of course the other a school shoe. Ties etc… forget it. *Neem* leaves and *pudina* leaves were out because such information was published in the newspaper, and for people who get up in the afternoon….the newspaper has already been trashed. So they were blissfully unaware of such international, national and local exhortations that TRYBY and TRYL were taking up so enthusiastically and which GOBY AND GORL did naturally – from VDFJ to learning Parandarese. They spent their time on stuff – like the Mac Lab PICSdad had set up: shuffles, Nanos, iPod and touch, iPad, iMac, MacBook + pro and a mac mini too. Playing games, writing apps. Working out on the obstacle course PICSdad had set up in his office. Stilt walking, rollerblading, unicycling, snorkeling, growing insectivorous plants and generally listening to music: rock and heavy metal to Senegalese mashups. Oh, and they tooled around with musical instruments: guitars, drums, tablas, and didgeridoos. They fought and won every debate, elocution, quiz, painting, collage competition that was around. They also loved these national science and math competitions and maxed them all the time. Hell, that's why the school didn't chuck them out, couldn't afford to. They Needed it for the school brochure.

They loved crazy stuff: COWBOY: fountain pens which he repaired for everyone; CORRAL, colors. Her prized colors were a set of powders from a wind-powered working windmill in the Netherlands which collected rocks from around the world and ground them into fantastic colors – you used them the same way cave people used them to paint madly, wildly and with abandon. Oh, she loved all animals including the nasty ones and is an animal whisperer of sorts.

And so what happened???

GOBY and GORL grew up and went to college. Free from all the rules, regulations, strictures, structures, frameworks, guidelines, edicts, diktats, control and commands at home, they simply couldn't handle freedom. Loose, free, free, liberated, unbound, unleashed, uncontrolled….. they quickly went downhill and couldn't complete college. Working as unskilled labor, they joined a labor union and their main recreation is fighting for more wages for lesser work. Nothing else is known about them.

TRYBY and TRYL took a year off after school went to a coaching center that taught them all the answers to questions they didn't understand and went to a top-class engineering school. They then took another year off to go to a coaching center that taught them by rote: more answers to more unintelligible questions, political correctness in a Group Discussion and Mom and Apple pie answers to an Interview. This got them into a top B-School. After graduating they married people like them. One sells soap and shampoo and the other – credit cards for *Kuttas*.[91] They had exactly 2.7 children each, bought one three-room flat each with access to a piddly swimming pool and a 20-meter jogging track. They also died exactly at 62 and 67 years of age in tandem with Government statistics.

COWBOY and CORRAL …ahhhhh. COWBOY set up an Apple help desk, runs a diving school and designs fountain pens and other fine writing instruments. He has also set up a media lab that explores the connection between humans and machines and how they exchange information. CORRAL set up several studios at NY, Santa Lucia, and Bahia Paraiso. She paints, sculpts and collects and catalogs music from around the world. She works with indigenous painters to bring their techniques and art out into the mainstream. She also runs a private zoo. Once in a while, they call PICS dad over when they have too much work to do. QED!!!!

[91] Dogs

The MUSTAKIN Story

Some science stuff makes people go bananas

Once upon a time, there was a farmer. His name was Mustakin. He was young, very hardworking and good-hearted. On a little farm that he had, he worked day and night to grow all kinds of vegetables. He grew pumpkin, squash, bitter gourd, carrot, snake gourd, elderberries, caper berries, elephant yam, colocasia, ash gourd, radish, potato, onion, drumstick and loads of other lovely vegetables.

A canal flowed just next to his farm. Mustakin knew all about fertilizers, trace minerals, pesticides, herbicides, good seeds, mulch, in short everything that an ace-farmer needs to know to crow crackin' good crops. So with his knowledge, good water from the canal and hard work, Mustakin was able to do very well indeed.

One day Bila and Kabun were cycling along the canal road. They were surprised to hear a great boo-hooing!!!!!

When they turned around the bend they almost fell off their bicycles – the boohooing was that LOUD.

So they stopped their cycles to look around and locate the epicenter of this boohooing. It was right inside Mustakin's farm. And the epicenter indeed was Mustakin himself who was making as much noise as a medium-sized hurricane. The bubbling volcano effect was Mustakin blowing and honking his nose into a kerchief.

Bila and Kabun stared at him in surprise!!!!!! And so they sat on either side of him on his *charpoy*[92] and asked him "Mustakin *bhaiya*[93], what happened?". They felt very bad for Mustakin and wanted to help him. He had been so nice to them, always giving them the freshest carrots, radishes, tomatoes and beetroots at the beginning of each season. Of course, Bila and Kabun would throw them carefully into the canal making sure that not a molecule of it reached home. They were very careful of their diet and always made sure that nothing ever contaminated it. Vegetables you see could seriously sully their diets of pizza, cola, potato chips, noodles and savory snacks. (yes potato is a vegetable but after it has been scared to death in boiling oil, it gives up being a vegetable – totally!!!!!).

And so Bila and Kabun sat on either side of Mustakin and asked him what the problem was. "Bo hooo booo huuuuhhuuu honk honky honk boo hoo" was his response. Once more they said to him, "Mustakin you are our friend, can we help you? What is the problem?" "Bo hooo booo huuuuhhuuu honk honky honk boo hoo" was his response

[92] Wood-rope-truss cot

[93] Brother

again. This went on till they had heard the "Bo hooo booo huuuuhhuuu honk honky honk boo hoo" explanation 34 times.

Then, exasperated, Bila and Kabun said to him "if you do not tell us properly this time, we are going to whack you with some carrots and radishes"!!!! And then poor Mustakin reduced the loudness of his boohooing and the honkiness of his honking and finally calmed down a little bit. "the crow birdies booo hooo hoo honky honk" – he started again. Being threatened with a large pumpkin over his head and a stout sugarcane on the side, Mustakin finally told them the whole story.

He has just planted some wonderfully expensive seeds – genetically modified seeds; they were GM. So EXPENSIVE. And the makers of the seeds said that his crops would be oh-so-good. And loads of protesters had tried to make the government stop them from selling them. "No Genetically Modified – GM seeds" they thundered. Silly geese they were. Every living thing on earth is genetically modified. Indeed, as Darwin told us in another great story, LIFE is about genetic modification. Even we are GM. We are the GM results of the biological love experiment of our parents. What the protesters meant was Genetically Engineered. But then you do not have to be logical and right. Just being LOUD will do. So while the LOUD HORDES were thundering, smart farmers like Mustakin quietly bought the seeds.

Just after he had planted the seeds properly in rows and columns, put a little bit of vermiculture around them and had watered them, a huge bunch of crows, a murder of crows as they are called, settled on his seedling plot and dug up and ate all the seeds. That was the day before. And yesterday too. And today as well - "Bo hooo booo huuuuhhuuu honk honky honk boo hoo" .... he started again. It really was murder: Mustakin's crying and the crows too.

On hearing this, Bila and Kabun went aside, did some major whispering, and some conspiratorial work: consisting of some thinking, consulting of their web-enabled iPod and iPad and then came to Mustakin and said: "We have the answer". We will make for you a monstrous anti-crow scarecrow!!!!!

So they gathered some bamboo sticks and some straw and after a fashion made a scarecrow. Then they told Mustakin that to make it realistic, they must put on it, Mustakin's own clothes. It should look like Mustakin, feel like Mustakin, sound like Mustakin and even smell like Mustakin. And so they made Mustakin take off his shirt and pant and banian[94] and chaddi[95]. Mustakin protested the banian and chaddi bit. But Bila and Kabun insisted – realism, credibility and authenticity, they chimed. Finally, Mustakin relented and took off everything. They gave Mustakin a banana leaf to cover his banana!!!!!

And then they recorded his "Bo hooo booo huuuuhhuuu honk honky honk boo hoo" and put it on a handy EPROM and connected it to speakers inside the scarecrow's head. The scarecrow was now complete. And then they went away.

The next day when they passed by the canal, Mustakin happily told them that when the crows came, they had

---

[94] Vest, somewhat like a **wife-beater** (yes, please check it out!!!!!!!!)

[95] Underwear

smirking faces and they flew down to the field. But when they saw the scarecrow and heard the awful noises it made, their murder became a mob, a riot and then sheer mayhem. And they fought each other to escape the sight of the terrible scarecrow and its god-awful banshee howling and the horrible smell too. And then Mustakin's field and seeds were safe...yippee!!!!!

And so Bila and Kabun left Mustakin smiling from ear to ear. But he couldn't wave a hearty goodbye to them for his banana leaves would fall down!!!!!!!

Just Tooling Around

It looked like there was, er, complete rebellion.

Zabeen's pen leaked and stained her shirt. Murad's cycle pedals kept falling off. Oindrila's glasses would flip-flop over her nose and if you know what spherical correction is – her world was upside down. Rishab's zipper malfunctioned and just as he was zipping up IT got stuck!!!! YEOW!!!!!! Dharti's Pants fell off when the belt buckle gave way and Dhara's toaster burnt her bread black!!! And all the I's, the i-pads, pods, and Macs; don't even talk about them. As it is they are pretty smart, but now they had become smart alecs indeed. Net connections to voice went to data; data went into storage and streamed into YouTube. Printers swallowed paper on command and the print outs mysteriously ended up on the toilet paper which equally strangely had glue on one side – whichever side you were interested in!

School compasses drew effortless triangles and foot rulers – zig-zag lines. Panni's pencil sharpener gave her perfect mushroom tips and Cooper got locked up INSIDE his bedroom. Pukar's study table kept rocking no matter how it was adjusted. Cynthia's knives hummed when cutting vegetables for a salad to take to school. The electricity kept flowing, like Thurber's Aunt prophesied, out of wall sockets onto floors and gave everyone a nasty shock at Parineet's midnight Birthday party.

The geysers in the bath gushed icy water and almost froze Piroze. School bags never closed properly and then wouldn't open – ask Sunaina and Cecil. Clothes in cupboards changed shelves all by themselves making Ronald and Jenny quite cross – for Jenny was in a pant and Ronald in a gay frock. The telephone rang and you could answer it only in the bath – from the telephone shower handle. The Landline telephone in the living room sprayed water!!!! Gurmit's television played all channels simultaneously making him quite dizzy. The FM radio in Parmeshwar's car kept playing "please fasten your seatbelts and do not go to the toilets. We shall be landing at New York shortly". The whole thing could have been brushed off as a series of coincidences. But when Dhurandhar went to buy a soft drink from the mall vending machine, matters came to a head. The vending machine asked him for a password, after swallowing his money. When Dhurandhar stared, stunned, the machine said: "if you have forgotten your password, please get your mother's permission with her digital signature verified by a first-class western bank.. now fasten your seatbelts, we are about to land…"….. Dhurandhar scooted as if a million ghouls were chasing him. Quickly he met Aditi, and Pheroze and Vinayak and Remit and Rhea and Renil….and all the others and the stories were the same. The machines were haunted, bewitched, under an evil spell and possessed.

So they asked Bila and Kabun. Here Kabun was of little help since she was the chief tester of the international society for destructive testing of equipment, stuff, machines, gadgets, things and whatchamacallits. Her recent testing experiment was "Canine Teeth vs. Mac cables, connectors and syncing cables". Round one, two and three had been overwhelmingly won by Mr. Morkley, her dog who had effortlessly converted many, many Mac cables to heart-rending 'I-trash".

But Bilan explained, calming the agitated, exasperated kids. No, no, it was not ghosts or poltergeists or spooks or all this X-files type of supernatural stuff. It was perfectly – logical, the "machines" were revolting. Against cruelty, irreverence, stupidity, negligence, disrespect and plain carelessness.

And he told them the story of *Vishwakarma*, the divine architect – inventor. He was indeed the progenitor of design, all things mechanical, architectural and the artifacts of the craftsman and worker – so the story goes. Indeed it was he who had gifted mankind[96] with the plough that made cultivation and settling down in one place possible, for the nomads that we were. During the *Vishwakarma puja*[97] ALL tools, implements, armaments, brushes, looms…indeed anything an engineer, craftsman, weaver or any professional uses is WORSHIPPED. During *Ayuthapuja*[98] falling in

---

[96] So the legend goes...

[97] Religious ceremony

[98] Literally - 'weapon/tool worship'

the first half of the waxing moon's period in *Navaratri*[99], all tools, books, scriptures and artifacts are cleaned, put on display, revered and prayed to. In modern times these have grown to include vehicles, computers, phones..indeed anything that amplifies human effort and reduces effort. *Lakshmi*[100] gifts the tools and artifacts, *Saraswati*[101] the skill and *Shakti*[102] blesses them. Owning a tool is not just a matter of acquisition: it also demands care, respect, repair, maintenance, detail and reverence.

Oooh said the kids, so that's a *Hindoo* (!) thing. "No," said Bilan, that's only one way to understand this. Every craftsman anywhere in the world worth his salt and skill has a special relationship with his tools, artifacts and skill. It is sacred and deep. It has been so through the ages for as long as anyone can remember.

For it can be the difference between life and death. A leaky kayak can kill an Inuit in freezing Arctic waters. A blowgun dart not sharpened and poisoned properly can lose the Amazon hunter a meal. A badly maintained baobab bark rope used by the Dogon to climb cliffs to harvest honey means plummeting to certain death. Poorly waxed sled runners means less speed and tired dogs on the Iditarod Husky Sled race. A loose horseshoe can unseat the rider and break a horse's leg. A jammed police gun can help a criminal run away. A dull blade can ruin a carpenter's work. A poorly

---

99 The festival of Nine Nights

100 The Hindu Goddess of Prosperity

101 The Hindu Goddess of Knowledge and Skill

102 The Hindu Goddess of Primordial Cosmic energy!!!!

sanded shuttle can damage a hugely expensive carpet on the loom. Faulty tuning can cost you the F1 race.

And so Bilan went on …tools…. artifacts…..care….. reverence……worship……..across the ages…and what were we now doing? Flinging their machines, wetting them in water….scratches all over…..no oiling their cycles, no maintenance, no polish, kick the vending machine….chuck the computer around….not even wipe it clean…put your sandwich on it….no cleaning, no wiping, no love, no care, no respect, no reverence, no worship. How long could the machines give performance, uncomplaining service, wait patiently at attention to help, take care not to hurt and above all deliver companionship beyond the call of duty??? And so they were tired, and bored, and disgusted and felt unwanted and so they revolted and how….!!!!!!!!!!!!!

And so the kids understood and from that day on every kid in their own way paid homage to every tool, artifact and skill they possessed. And the machines forgave them became amongst their best friends.

ZOO Mein Mangal[103]

This is a zoo story. Literally: zoo means animals and this is what the story is about. And this is a story about a zoo that has MAX species. So you would be forgiven for thinking that this story is in the USA or some such fancy country. You are WRONG: well partly wrong.....The USA has the best zoos in the world; collectively; Australia and other countries, especially Singapore have very good ones; African countries have great Wildlife viewing opportunities; Brazilian rainforests are rich..... but here hold your breath......................... .... India, kilo for kilo, animal for animal has the MOST species in the world. NAMDAPHA in Arunachal Pradesh is the ONLY National Park in the world with four BIG cats: Snow LEOPAD, Clouded Leopard, Panther and Tiger. Also in a BIG BIG WHAMMY, India is the ONLY place in the world to have Lions, Rhinos Tigers, Buffalo, Leopard,

[103] Sort of means, nice auspicious things

Species of Crocs – Mugger and Gharial, River Otters and Dolphins and Elephants..(the Sumatran/Javan rhino, Sri Lankan Elephant are too small in number to count-actually we worry about them rather than watch them.).

But our zoos are very very good. So good that we will not talk about them. Instead, we will talk about a zoo that could be. After all, in a story, we can do a story inside!!!!!!!!!!!!!!!!!!!!!

So here was a zoo of our dreams with ALLL the Indian Animals. And there were otters and lions, tigers, panthers, clouded leopards, snow leopards, fishing cats, honey badgers, elephants, ant eaters, rhinos, eagle owls, river dolphins, pythons, king cobras, rat snakes, snakes of a hundred kinds, chital, sambhar, gaur, gibbons, macaques, mahseers, peacocks, monitor lizards, wasps of twenty kinds, spiders, snails, butterflies and crocodiles and gharials and too many animals to name. Tons of them.

And all these animals were in their enclosures. And they were sick and tired of people troubling them, poking them, throwing stones at them, feeding them and generally making their lives hell. That's life in an Indian Zoo.

So the animals decided they needed to have fun. And so one night they made a plan...........

Many school children groups, NGOs, college groups etc kept coming to the zoo, perhaps enticed by the ULTRA low entry fee and their chance to trouble some animals which JUST cannot attack them........ and the fact that they have a picnic after which they can monstrously litter the place.

So this day the students from Ancientben – Hoarypast-Sethji Malikji School were on their field trip. Little did they know that the ANIMALS had already made a "Plan"!!

The Ancientben – Hoarypast-Sethji Malikji School authorities had made a plan that all students would submit a "nature study" to their science class teachers. And this would be sent to some 'sister' USA school/institution/museum… The poor US Schoolchildren having never heard of Honey Badger or Pangolin would immediately say "what an exotic project", which the Ancientben – Hoarypast-Sethji Malikji School would immediately use in their Brochure next year to lure more unsuspecting students to join their uninspiring school………..

So the students were on their field trip……

They were in groups and observing and these were their observations:

- Otters have group discussion in the morning and they make their fish swim as if they were doing an item number before they eat them
- Bats wash their food before they eat it.
- Peacocks dance with the insects before they put them in their insect collection.
- Badgers "pee" on their vegetables before they eat them.
- Langurs make their tails into 'springs' and then sit on them.
- Rhinos sharpen their horns with pencil sharpeners
- Elephants do yoga with their trunks
- Rabbits eat Red Raw meat, grilled.
- Clouded leopards hang upside down
- Owls use spectacles to see better…

- Termites use hand sanitizer to clean up
- Langurs use cell phones to communicate
- Fishing cats use rods and reels to fish
- King cobras use iPods to listen to music.
- River dolphins use sun block cream and moisturizers to keep fresh…

And the students gave all these reports to the teachers. And the teachers being so underpaid and overworked at the Ancientben – Hoarypast-Sethji Malikji School just collated them and sent them to the Great Big Institution in the USA without once checking them. And the poor American children believed the zoo observations and thought them true. And being generous Americans they soon organized drives and campaigns.

- "Cellphones for Monkeys" drive.
- Do not throw away your old pencil sharpeners – some Indian Rhinos could use them!!!!
- Donate old spectacles for owls
- Give us your junk mp3 players for King Cobras

And you know what the American public thought of these efforts……

That's why the USA now believes that apart from being 'Bangalored'[104] it has also been "^%Y**^&^ ^U^("!!!!!!!!!!!!!!!!!!!

---

[104] An American expression that means losing one's job to an outsourced company, usually one located in Bangalore!

The Tooth Fairy BPO

The tooth fairy is a legend all kids KNOW is true!!!

When kids are 5 or 6 or 7 or more ….their teeth, oh their teeth. What happens is that their 'milk' teeth fall off and new 'adult' ones take their place. Now, this is fairly unsettling for kids. Well, to see themselves in the mirror and look like they have become grandmothers or something with missing teeth. And the worst thing is that the front teeth which are the most visible, fall off first!!!!!

And so here comes the tooth fairy. Legend has it that if kids wrap up their fallen tooth in a piece of paper or cotton and keep it under their pillows, the Tooth Fairy will visit them. When they go to sleep, then something magical happens. The next morning when they wake up, the tooth is gone but there is some nice money under the pillow. Yippeeeee!!!!

And so the tooth fairy was busy doing this every night – take old teeth, bless the children, leave money, and rush off to the next house. What she did with the teeth is **not** another story. She used them and her magical powers to make more teeth. So if one of yours fell off, she would take it and make the next one for you.

And so this tooth fairy business started in, naturally, once upon a time, in a far far away land. But what happened is that children in other countries also started to believe in the tooth fairy. And so the poor tooth fairy kept rushing to and fro from far far away land to country after country and back and forth and could hardly get a moment of sleep.

She went and hired a management consultant to advise her. Enter Kolaa Raoo!!!! He said, "pooh what you need to do is to outsource your Business Processes". And the poor Tooth Fairy who was already short of time grew more frantic. What was this Business Process Outsourcing, she had no clue? And did the idea have teeth in it??[105]

And Kolaa Raoo explained. The Tooth Fairy was a great concept and this tooth for money was a great business model. What the Tooth Fairy needed to do was to concentrate on building the Brand, and get more kids in more countries to believe in the Tooth Fairy. Thus more teeth, more countries and yippee one day they could go IPO - Incisor Proliferation Opportunity.... The only hitch was that this reach under the pillow, pull out old teeth, put money and vanish was routine and boring and someone else should do it - Process Outsourcing.

And so Aurkixgen Xizwqyant – the famous BPO company was given the contract. Note the name. This is important. ALL BPO companies must have a name like this. A whiff of Greek or better, Norse mythology plus

---

[105] Pun intended!!

letters no one can use in Scrabble, like QWZX and ending in something that sounds like a recombinant DNA drug. This guarantees your business like nothing else.

Now Aurkixgen Xizwqyant was no slowcoach. It went to work right away. And so they used GPS and GIS and handheld computers to make work more efficient. A hub and spoke system was established to collect teeth and disburse money. And all was hi-tech and hi-speed and humming along.

The people at Aurkixgen Xizwqyant were smart. In fact, extra smart. They figured that this idea of putting cash under pillows was suboptimal. After all, kids lose, what, 7 or ten or twelve teeth. Now why lay out cash every time. It would be easier to transfer it digitally to a bank account. So kids now were flabbergasted. Their tooth under the pillow was gone but in its place was a 6-page application form to open an account at the tooth fairy bank!!!!

And to make matters smoother the folks at Aurkixgen Xizwqyant figured that they needed to track children accurately. After all, the six-year-old who lost a tooth looked very different when she was eight and lost a molar. So they had to track. The result – flabbergasted kids again who woke up to find a barcode, screen printed on their forehead the morning after they had stashed a broken tooth under their pillow.

The Tooth Fairy now had a great brand name and more and more children in more and more countries were getting fond of her. Now, these were the ones she handled before transferring them over to Aurkixgen Xizwqyant. What happened to them after she transferred them to the BPO.... read on...

Meanwhile, the folks at Aurkixgen Xizwqyant had a brainwave. Apart from teeth what was the other stuff that people disposed of off when they grew? Ok nails cut, hair cut… so why not start associated, diversified businesses? Flabbergasted children again now found nails cut to the quick, whether boys or girls. Wake up and find your fancy hairdo is now a military crew cut.

Soon the Tooth Fairy outsourcing company Aurkixgen Xizwqyant was making kids' lives all over the world miserable:

To make the process faster operatives started PULLING out children's teeth. Efficient process you see- why wait for them to become loose, pull them ALL off, instead of waiting for them under the pillow after they fell off.

Hair cutaway ruining hairstyles

Nails cutaway ruining nail adornment

All this meant they made more and more money. After all, just the tooth business got them so little. This was pay dirt and the tooth fairy would soon become their biggest client.

This was bad enough. But when kids saw that some of the keys from their computers and gamepads and cell phones were missing, they threw up a ruckus. THE BPO Aurkixgen Xizwqyant people were taking away keys like QWZKX to put on their signboards and letterheads and so on as part of a cost reduction exercise.

So the kids hatched a plan….all kids informed each other and their plan was ready.

Six of them who really had a tooth fallen off gathered at one house. They lay six pillows on the bed and put their teeth under them. And they hid under the bed.

At night when the Aurkixgen Xizwqyant people came, the kids quickly took them by surprise and covered their heads with pillow covers. Then they replaced the company name on their badges with another that read "Ghasitaram Outsourcewala"

Other kids placed the barcode scanners on crazy stuff they got. Like: noodle bags, detergent packs, dog food, and even toilet paper.

In the handheld devices of the Aurkixgen Xizwqyant Company, now Ghasitaram Outsourcewalla, they wrote "hare" instead of "hair". "Carpentry Nails" instead of nails and "alphabet soup" instead of soup.

And when they changed "tooth" to "toot" and "teeth" to "tithe" it was the beginning of the end. And thousands of kids had done the same things to other Aurkixgen Xizwqyant agents that night.

And then the fun started. First of all the Aurkixgen Xizwqyant warehouses were now full of hares hopping all around. There were also tons of earthmovers, detergent packs, noodles, dog food, notebooks, in fact, anything that could have a barcode tag was now in the warehouse ready for shipment to the Tooth Fairy. Meanwhile, thousands of liters of alphabet soup were mucking up the place.

The Tooth Fairy was disgusted with the container loads of all this nonsense she now received. She had been getting hair and brand-new teeth and XZGWQ bits and pieces.

She was convinced that if Aurkixgen Xizwqyant was such a large operation, some small mistakes would occur. But the sight of hares driving earthmovers amidst the slush of alphabet soup was just too much. Besides the tooting of a thousand horns, the Government had imposed a tax on her (remember the tithe!!???)

She called them up. "Good morning, Ghasitaram Outsourcewallah HQ, how may we help you?" was the reply and the Tooth Fairy's teeth almost fell out. Zip zap zoom she fired them and warned them never to come near a kid ever again anywhere in the world. And all the alphabet soup was to pour into the orifices sorry offices of Kolaa Raoo, the accursed Management Consultant. And she got back to her work and from that day all was well and everyone lived happily ever after.

By the way, the change of name proved to be disastrous for Aurkixgen Xizwqyant. Ghasitaram Outsourcewallah was impossible for their clients and all of moved their business to KUQZObane ZAXMOKene.

The tooth fairy managed to clean her office and home and garden. But then what was she to do with all the stuff? The alphabet soup was gone, but the rest of the stuff???

So ever so once in a while, a kid will be flabbergasted. Instead of money under the pillow, there might be a hare, a packet of noodles, a cake or soap or oopppsss, a massive earthmover!!!!!! NOW YOU KNOW WHY?!!!!!!!!

Ultrasonic Bills[106]

Once upon a time, there was a lovely Labrador Retriever – a BIG black one. He looked oh-so-fierce and black and massive but was actually a cootchie pie.

And he loved children, he loved playing and above all he loved retrieving – remember he was a Labrador Retriever.

When this breed was 'developed' it was as a Hunting Dog. 'Sportsmen" would shoot ducks and other waterfowl with guns. But they were too sissy poo to wade into deep water So the brave retrievers would go and get the 'downed' birds. And they were mighty trained. They would stand on three legs, tail pointing to the 'sportsman' and the free leg 'pointing' to the bird. Then they would go and fetch!!!!!!

So such a dog called Ronnie was living in a 'bungalow'. Now 'bungalow' is a British term that means a LARGE house with SUBSTANTIAL grounds where even a horse could romp around and get somewhat tired. But 'bungalow'

106 A story well into science fiction!

has now come to mean a house which has a boundary wall ('not a flat' would be a more accurate description).

So Ronnie, let it be said had very kind 'masters'. One girl and two boys and two parents. But all were busy in one place or the other... And doing something or the other. Basically to keep the payments on their 'bungalow' and two cars and two scooters going. And poor Ronnie was at home all alone, almost all the time. Remember he is a HUNTING dog and is 'designed' to be outdoors and action-oriented. Once in a while, they would take him out to potty but that was it....

So poor Ronnie would fetch a ball once in a while and then sleep. To their master's (mistresses) credit it must be said that he got ALL the food he wanted and more. But the excitement of being a hunting dog was totally missing.....

So poor Ronnie jammed up with Bila and Kabun. Bila was the technical guy and Kabun was the Animal expert!!!!!! She loved animals and he loved technology. So they formed a team: Bilan Kabun and Ronnie.

Now hearing, human hearing is between 20 and 20,000 cycles a second, but hold it, that is perfect human hearing.....very very few people have it. But dogs have ultrasound hearing, so do bats and porpoises and, wait for it, humpbacked whales..... And at the other end of the spectrum is infrasound. Elephants with 'infrasound', the stuff that makes your belly and your surroundings resonate.....and your pajjies[107] fly off....

So Bila and Kabun set up a Mac-based electronic-internet based real-time sound network. Porpoises, Humpbacked

---

[107] (Pyjamas)

whales, Bats and elephants all contributing real-time to a sophisticated mixer.....

So the 'Team' got to work. To 'help'!!! And Ronnie who wanted to roam around got to work.

So the next day Ronnie went to work on his family's bills. The parents were rudely woken up one night at two by the cellular company bill collector who said "*ben have be lakh na bill thaye che toh advance aapo pade*[108]" (our bill is Rs 2,00,00 and you have to pay up an advance)... and the family were stunned. Ronnie had figured out the rf frequencies and the nearby bat which was hiding in Bila/ Kabun's house had figured out the modulation and had changed the bill. When the family protested, they were presented with an actual bill that listed hour-long calls to Norway, Scott station in the Arctic and various calls to Antarctic ice stations, Chile, Nicaragua and even some to Senderoso Luminoso (the dreaded Chilean terrorist group)!!!!!!!!!!!!!!!!!!! So they paid up! Shhh!!!

Next time the family went to the Fuel Station, the only time the dog got to travel, the fuel station guy used his handheld computer. Helped by the bat, Ronnie made the bill some Rs. 18,000!!!! When the family protested "how can we buy 300 liters of fuel, the pump guy said," you must be terrorists with secret fuel tanks to store arms and explosives". And so the family quietly paid up. Shhhhsh!

And when they went to the local fast food drive by counter and ordered for a meal their bill came to Rs. 26,000 aided by the porpoise's audio recording!!!! And the family

---

[108] Your bill is now Rs 200,000 and you will have to pay us an advance if you want service continued!!

were flabbergasted, two burgers and French fries with one soda for Rs. 26,000!!!!!!!!!!!!!!!!

And then when the electricity bill came in the family's collective pajjis flew off. Rs. 13,34,500 …..ooooh. Ronnie had just used the porpoises and the bat's ultrasonic responses using his small device to alter the meter reader's device!!!!!!!!!!!!! The meter reader wanted to know what banned information transmission devices the family was using that consumed so much electricity? Were they the local hub for transmitting WIKILEAKS in Terabytes? And before he told the Police would they pay up? They quietly did.

This way Ronnie freaked out on the family's cellular, electricity, fuel, supermarket and other bills. And when they would sleep he would use the family's sound system to playback the elephant's rumbling infra-sound to make the whole building tremble as if it was an earthquake!!! And the whole family would run outside the house and Ronnie could play all night outside!!!!!!!!!!!!!!!!

And by the way, the family paid up sooooooo much that they couldn't afford to live in the 'bungalow' and were camped in the society's common garden. Ronnie had a great time but the family would have been better off having a cat…..

Pics Dad Plays Judo!!!

And so PICS (Politically Incorrect Children's Stories) dad was wondering about his Bila and Kabun. Is it ever possible to get these guys to toe the line, behave, conduct themselves, and build character…..???? After all, he had been trying for so many years. And his kids kept presenting *fait accompli, ceterus paribus, habeas corpus* and if all else failed then cute faces and a hug….

All rules/systems/processes were subverted right after inception.

For instance

- PICS Dad came back from a tour and the kids wanted a leave-of-absence letter for school that morning, immediately. (RULE: *I must know why you take leave BEFORE you take leave….)*
- Pencils NOW (at 6.30 am) or we cannot go to the exam. (*RULE: We must always plan in advance and not leave anything for the last moment….)*

- Please, please can we sleep for 10 minutes more and then miss the bus and then you drop us to school... *(RULE: We should be environmentally conscious (go by bus) and also conserve, for example – fuel)*
- Oh, today we have to take lunch boxes with us, 5 minutes before they leave *(RULE: If you need lunch tomorrow tell me today, not 5 minutes before the bus comes in).*

He wondered if this mayhem was ever going to end. And so he dreamt up an idea if you cannot beat them, join them and use a little judo in the bargain. Judo in the sense, use the opponent's strength against them!!!!!!

And so he set to work. Next time the kids came in with a request for a leave letter[109], PICSdad chose them this from a collection of leave letters. Note the subtle Judo-Esque vectors at work here:

a. the kids are in a hurry
b. they present their request at the last minute hoping for a quick and lenient treatment
c. Being in a hurry, they are unlikely to read it before turning it in!!!!
d. BINGO!!!!!

And so here are the letters....!!!!!!!!!!

[109] A note that school requires to authorize 'leave-of-absence'

Letter – 01

Dear Class Teacher,

I was away on tour and have been asked to provide a leave letter for Saturday when I was not even here. So here it is, full of mendacity, fabrication, subtle deception and hyperbole:

Bilan had a stomachache

Thanking you

Yours, brightly insincerely
PICS dad

Letter – 02

To: Her Highness 'The Class Teacher", Order-of-the-red-pencil, Commander-of-the-assembly-ground

From: PICS dad

Saturday, the 23rd of March, 2012 AD dawned as usual. The cocks crowed, the flowers bloomed and the air was full of pregnant silence. I have it on the authority of Jeeves and Mr. Wooster that the lark was on the wing, the snail was on the thorn and all was well with the world.

Verily no one could have dreamt of the incredible epic saga about to unfold, the dramatic events of which have been captured in my trilogy, soon to be published and made available in reputed bookshops to discerning readers like you.

The central protagonists in this event were none other than Bilan and Kabun, but if I elaborated, I would spoil your suspense. Please grant them leave of absence for Saturday without asking why, and you will get a special discount of 25% on all the three books!!!!

Thanking you

Yours Sincerely

Letter – 03

Please Destroy **Before Reading!!!!!!** Top Secret

To: Codename: Ponderous Borer[110] – The Class Teacher

From: Agent Falcon, Operation Peregrine

Dear Ponderous Borer,

He who cannot be mentioned was involved on Saturday on a matter of the highest national security. At the express request of the President of India, please make sure that 'HIS' attendance is marked 'present' so that his alibi is secure and his cover remains intact.

Do not ask questions. Do not confiscate his weapons and body armor. Above all act normal.

Tear this letter, put it in your mouth, chew and swallow it. Potty in a public toilet and flush repeatedly so that this communication cannot be reconstructed. You have been warned....

unsigned, for obvious reasons......

---

110 The Ponderous Borer – *(Ergatus spiculatus)* the real name of a real beetle. A big one, it 'bores' into Pine trees and is quite a pest. The name is too cute not to apply to people!!!!

Letter – 04

Dear Class Teacher,

Please grant Bilan and Kabun leave of absence for Saturday since our family was celebrating International Nudists Day and they were a little embarrassed to come to school with only backpacks.

Regards

PICSDAD

Letter – 05

To: The Class Teacher

From: PICS dad

Dear Madam,

Due to the rainy season, Bilan's and Kabun's complete attire, including the unmentionables, of which they have very few, were in a comparative state of hi-humidity. This situation was further exacerbated by the paucity of solar radiation. Hence to preclude the possibility of their epidermis forming a habitat for certain microscopic botanical and zoological specimens, it was decided by the residential top management, with enthusiastic approval from your students, that attendance at places of education be shifted from mandatory to optional. This has been immediately implemented.

Please concur and collaborate without prejudice.

Thanking you profusely

PICS dad

And on the day when Mr. Morkley, our dog **ACTUALLY** ate their homework....

Letter – 06

Dear Teacher,

I do not have the time to invent anything better.

Please excuse Bila and Kabun for not submitting their homework today.

Dog ate it!!!!!!

Regards

With sinful glee…...!!!!!!!!!!

PICS dad

Letter – 07

To: The class teacher

From: PICS dad

Sub: Kabun's absence from class on Saturday

Dear Teacher,

It was like this. For some reason, still not clear at the moment, Kabun decided to have a bath on Saturday morning. Her mother then dried and oiled her hair and then Kabun went to the full-length mirror in our guest room to comb and plait her hair (really).

When she looked in the mirror, maybe because of the oil or (most likely) because of the bath, she saw a stranger she did not recognize. A loud scream was followed by even louder crashes – which was Kabun pulverizing the mirror with a golf club.

Kabun now believed the stranger had been subdued and was waiting near the mirror frame, golf club handy to handle any more unwanted intrusions.

She slept only on Sunday morning after the frame was sold to the local kabadiwallah[111].....

Please give her leave of absence and do allow her, her golf club in the classroom.......

Regards

PICS dad

---

[111] This is a fantastic Indian system in which itinerant salesmen (haven't seen a woman yet) pick up recyclable paper, plastic, bottles, etc from houses and pay for them!

Letter – 08

To: The class teacher

From: PICS dad

Sub: Leave of absence

Dear Teacher,

My children, both Apple Adepts, believe they have downloaded an App that allows their teacher to believe they are in class while they are snoozing at home.

They have been testing it out since Saturday and I guess this misguided belief will persist for some time.

Please give an indefinite leave of absence.

Regards

PICS dad.

PS: there may be a huge market for an app that gets to slimy kid's Apple machines that makes them believe that missing school will permanently fry their computers and make them incredibly attractive to the opposite sex (my kids are small enough to HATE this idea, so it should work)

Letter – 09

Ahmedabad
April 2, 2012

Dear Teacher,

I have forgotten the excuses, lame truths, half-truths, webs of deceit, shams, guile and plain lies that I have used in the past for leave-of-absence letters. And I am all mixed up.

So please select an unused one from this list. Better still let me know which are unused so I can use them in the future...use for Bila, Kabun or both.

Getting Up Late Set

A. B/K set 3 alarms on different devices for different times,

   a. Get up and go by bus
   b. Get up a little late, and ask PICS dad to drop by car
   c. Too late to go.
   d. They missed the time sequence and got up late...

B. The a/c setting was on ultra-low leading B/K to believe that they were on holiday in Leh, Ladakh. So they got up late.

C. His underwear slipped down to his feet tripping him in the night when he was going to the washroom. Through some incredible coincidence, this changed the page on his calendar leading him to believe it was a Sunday... (even I do not believe I am actually writing this)

D. Mr. Morkley was licking her feet as she slept leading her to believe she was undergoing Kerala Ayurveda massage… and so she overslept, not wanting to interrupt therapy.

TECHNICAL: Computers, Plumbing, Combs, etc…

A. He had a bath and all drains clogged up…. So he couldn't……

B. He discovered soap and its properties; unfortunately, the pH of the soap did not match the TDS of the water and he was unable to wash it off….so he could not…

C. She discovered an innovative use of the Comb – to comb hair and combed so much that the static electricity on her body zapped the access codes on all our doors. She was unable to get out in time so ……

D. He participated in a strictly unofficial drinking glass – vacuum competition. This consists of placing a drinking glass around your lips and generating so much vacuum that the glass will not fall off – for as long as possible. This left such a red band around his mouth that it looked as if he had been around lipstick laden lips for a whole evening. To avoid embarrassment……

Philosophical

A. He ended up so neat and clean and dashing and handsome that all the girls of the society would not let him go. All the running away, escape maneuvers, etc left him so tired that he was unable....

B. They realized the futility of education and the impossibility of this rat race and was so ......that they could not....

C. Having won a Spelling Bee, he developed WASP tendencies and demanded a series of student rights... most of which neither your school nor we can provide. The debate took so long that he was not able....

D. Having had a proper bath, and having found shoes, socks, uniform, belt, tie, blazer, badge and having packed their bags correctly, with their lunch boxes and water bottles ready and in time for the bus with homework all done Bila and Kabun were so stunned, they were sure they were in a bizarre dream-real life, Kafka–inception type of simulation and refused to go to....

Letter – 10

To: Class Teachers, Bilan and Kabun's

From: PICS dad

Sub: Leave of absence

Dear Teacher,
Please grant me a permanent leave of absence. Surrender. I give up. TATA

Regards
PICS dad

----------------------------EOF----------------------------------

CPSIA information can be obtained
at www.ICGtesting.com
Printed in the USA
BVHW031358270120
570624BV00001B/1

9 781647 607838